EVA ALTON

THE VAMPIRE'S ASSISTANT

The Vampires of Emberbury Series

Praise for Eva Alton's Books:

"Combines the best of the paranormal genre with
the best of romance."

"I would read it a thousand times over."

"An incredibly original and unique take on
vampires and witches. It dazzled me
from beginning to end."

"I read it every spare moment I had.
Engaging, entertaining, and utterly captivating...
You won't be able to put it down
until the very end."

Other books by Eva Alton:

The Vampires of Emberbury Series
Stray Witch
Witch's Mirror
Witches' Masquerade
Witches' Elements
A Winter's Cobalt Kiss
The Vampire's Assistant

Witches of Ibiza Series:
Iris – The Witch's Blood Spell
Selena – Wolf Moon
Mina – Spirits of Shadows

Historical Fantasy
Hidden Notes

THE VAMPIRE'S ASSISTANT

"That's the point I'm coming to," said Sancho.
"And now tell me, which is the greater work,
to bring a dead man to life or to kill a giant?"

"The answer is easy," replied Don Quixote,
"it is a greater work to bring to life a dead man."

The History of Don Quixote
Miguel de Cervantes Saavedra

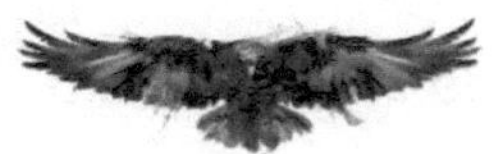

Prologue

Francesca

Summer 1981

I only kill those who wish to die.

When I saw Julia Reighton for the first time, not long after the latest war, she was kneeling over an empty tomb with dewy eyes. War widows were often resilient little creatures, but that one seemed too lost to bounce back, which in turn, made her an ideal candidate for one of my charity projects.

After the war, Saint Emery's graveyard became one of my favorite places to spend the evenings and pursue what I liked to call *conscientious hunting*. The cemetery was small and enchanting, just like the one at home; but unlike our homely Saint Anne's, which had been abandoned for at least a century, Saint Emery was always bursting with grieving souls who often converted willingly into limp, guiltless victims.

Little did I know that behind Julia Reighton's defeated façade inhabited a fierce individual who would change the way our clan had lived up to that very day.

The unexpected advent of that rare human specimen gifted me with a daughter and a sister.

But robbed me of a brother.

It would take me a long time to come to terms with Julia's paradox, and had I known the turmoil she carried with her, I might have consummated my plans and executed her that very night without a second thought.

But Ludovic didn't let me, and that was how we ended up sheltering an ancient rival's blood under the vaults of The Cloister.

Chapter 1

Julia

Emberbury, July 1946

> *"My name is Julia, and I am a widow.*
> *Just another war widow."*

Looking at the leather-bound diary, I stared at those perturbing words, then crossed them out in a fit of rage. Memories of Gabriel's useless funeral flooded my mind, and the pressure inside my chest threatened to make my heart explode.

The thought of explosions made me even angrier, as it reminded me of Gabriel's demise. Hastily, I sought the pendant around my neck. The cold, grounding metal sent me back to the present and to the mahogany bureau desk I was sitting at. The room where I was penning my thoughts was windowless but lavishly decorated: just a small part of a secret underground dwelling beneath a graveyard, which I now called my home. My mind traveled to the day when everything had started: that evening I had been given a choice between serving the dead and joining their ranks.

I had chosen the former.

***

Saint Emery, 4 months earlier.

A dozen black roses adorned the carved granite headstone in Saint Emery's cemetery. It was getting late, but I wasn't the only woman kneeling in front of the cold stone on just another post-war evening.

I was young and free, with a future in front of me. The return of peace was supposed to bring our lives back to *normal*. Normal or not, I didn't care much for whatever the future might bring, especially not now that Gabriel was gone forever.

Visiting his tomb was a source of unexpected satisfaction, and sometimes I wondered whether I was more in love with the ghost than I had been with the man himself. I had known Gabriel for such a brief time before his deployment that memories blended with imaginings in an indivisible whole. Did I love *him* or his memory? It was hard to decide, since my fondness for darkness dated back to my childhood, to the day my baby brother and mother had died in childbirth. Back then, I had become fascinated with death and its eerie choices. Gabriel's memory had just given me leeway to commune with those demons guiltlessly. Nobody blamed a widow for her hopelessness in 1946.

The rest of the grieving women gradually left. After darkness fell, I was the only one to remain on the graveyard grounds. I liked to stay until closing time, because that gave me the freedom to talk aloud to my deceased husband. Obviously, he never answered, but it was easier to cry when nobody was watching.

"Gabriel, if only I could see you again," I murmured, lighting a candle and trying to remember the last time we'd been together. They had sent him abroad soon after our wedding, and he had soon after become yet another piece of collateral damage. "I wish I could be reunited with you."

"I could help you with that," someone answered.

Startled, I jolted on the spot. *Had the angel statues answered my plea? Or had it been… Gabriel's ghost?*

But it had been none of those: just a tiny young woman, who was standing right behind me.

I hadn't seen her around Saint Emery before, but she looked just like another one of us: yet another girl who lost a loved one to the horror: a husband, a father, a brother… maybe all of those at the same time. This lady might look wealthier than the regular widows who hovered around Saint Emery, but I had learned that death wasn't picky with its subjects.

"Do we know each other?" I asked her, taking in her eccentric clothes, which might have come straight from my grandmother's closet. She had long, blond hair, rolled up and pinned with care, and it glistened mysteriously in the light of the many lit candles of the graveyard. Something in her bearing told me she came from money, unlike me.

"Does our acquaintance matter, as long as I'm willing to help you?" Her smile reminded me of the funerary sculptures around us: oddly heavenly, but leaning toward irrational. She spoke with a sweet, slight Italian accent. "If you want to meet your husband again, I have a way to provide what your heart longs for."

"My dear lady, whoever you are, you are not above God, and I doubt you can raise the dead."

I stood up, offended by her insolent interruption. I'd come back tomorrow, once she was gone.

"I didn't speak of raising the dead, but of helping you meet them, *signora*."

"Excuse me, but I don't like the turn this conversation is taking," I said angrily, wiping my still damp eyes on my sleeve. The girl looked harmless, so reedy and small, but her sense of humor wasn't much to my liking. I didn't feel like being made fun of or arguing, so I postponed my grieving for the next day and left.

Gabriel certainly wouldn't mind the waiting.

That was one of the advantages of having

dates with dead people. That, and they rarely contradicted you.

They were good listeners, too.

As I crossed the gates of the cemetery and left Gabriel's tomb behind, I could still feel the blonde woman's presence behind me, like a haunting, dark shadow.

I reached the path which led to my home. It ran through a small thicket, and I hesitated. Taking the route through the woods would mean a shorter walk back home from the cemetery; but in the darkness, and with a bizarre woman following me, it might be safer to take the main road. Postwar life was hard, and robbery wasn't so uncommon.

As I stepped onto the cobblestones, a small hand grabbed my neck. Another one covered my mouth and dragged me into the woods, with implausible efficiency. I tried to resist, but the arms which held me were like a steel cage. I kicked and fought, but the stranger didn't even flinch.

I saw her face: it was the girl from the graveyard. With an iron embrace, she pinned me against a tree and I started to shake.

"You still haven't answered my question," she said, uncovering my mouth. Her smile left me speechless: sharp, ivory fangs protruded between her carmine lips. "I think we can assist each other."

Her eyes flashed with a tinge of red. By then, I was completely light-headed. She started to unbutton my coat and her lips approached my neck with surprising tenderness. My body went limp in her arms against my will.

"Francesca, stop!" A male voice approached us in the darkness and the girl turned around.

A stranger appeared behind me. His features were reminiscent of the girl's, but in a more tanned version; his choice of attire was as peculiar as hers. While the female looked very young, the male newcomer might have been in his late twenties, maybe thirties.

"You just want her for yourself, brother," the woman spat, reluctant to release me.

"Her scent is strange," the man answered sternly. "Dangerous."

I gasped as his fiery gaze sent shivers down my spine. Me, a penniless widow, dangerous?

"No worse than those putrid soldiers we used to feast on during the war," the blonde girl answered with indifference. "I found her first, so she's mine now."

They spoke as though I wasn't even there. The woman held me against the tree trunk with just one hand and the man stood behind her, his hands on his hips.

"Francesca, you know the rules."

The man paced left and right. A long, velvet cloak swayed behind him like a flag.

"I do. That's why. She implied she wanted to die. There's nothing illegitimate in my actions."

"It might be a trap, *sorellina mia*. It definitely

smells like one. Remember. Remember what…"

"No, Ludovic," she whispered, and they exchanged a chaste kiss. "Leave her to me."

The man pushed his companion aside and pulled gently at the lapels of my woolen coat, inspecting the skin around my neck with a mixture of scientific interest and distressed intensity. He caressed my throat with ice-cold fingers, and his face inched toward mine, just like a lover's. I flinched, almost expecting him to steal a kiss, but he only sniffed the skin behind my ear, then winced with disgust. "There's no doubt. She's a—"

The woman interrupted him, "She's not—despite her scent, she has no power, no aura, can't you sense it?"

He nodded reluctantly and let go of my coat, but clutched my arm with no visible intention of letting me go.

"Now she's seen too much, anyway," the woman said, brushing a thumb over my cheek with odd longing.

"We can remedy that. Allow me to make her forget and let's go."

"Even her kind deserves mercy, Ludovic!"

"This is not about mercy! This is about my sister's safety."

"I can take care of myself. Of both of us."

"That you can," the man agreed, bowing his head. "But these charity projects of yours will soon cost you your immortal life."

She smiled at him sweetly, and I glimpsed a trace of benevolence beneath those madness-stricken eyes.

"This woman poses no risk to any of us. She's not Bellissa. The difference between us, brother, is that I still haven't lost faith in true goodness. I kept an empathy for those in grief, no matter where they came from. We both know the pain of mourning a loved one. Even so, can you fathom the sorrow of weeping over an empty grave?"

An empty grave, she said.

How could she know that?

Suddenly, the blonde perked up and tilted her head, making golden waves of hair cascade down her left shoulder. "I have a wonderful idea. Maybe you are right, and she doesn't seek that kind of mercy. But we could still use her for our own benefit."

"*Use* her!" the man said with shock, "How does one make use of a—"

"*Shh*, brother. Maybe it's better if she doesn't know just yet." She put an index finger to his lips, which were surprisingly red. "And to answer your question: in a number of ways."

She giggled mischievously.

"No," he stomped the ground with frustration.

"Oh, but Elizabeth will be thrilled. It will be our little present for her."

"*Cara mia…*" He shook his head. "I hope you

know what you are doing."

"Maybe we should just ask her."

The man buttoned my coat with startling dexterity. Then he shook me lightly, as if to wake me up from the shock which had overcome me.

"Excuse my sister," he said, waving towards the blonde and looking deeply into my eyes. His were a strange shade of azure and shone vividly under the moonlight with otherworldly incandescence. He looked dazzling, but utterly terrifying at the same time. "Would you or wouldn't you like to die tonight?"

That may be the strangest question anyone had ever asked me up to that day.

And despite my grief, despite all the tears shed for Gabriel, and despite the desperation which had choked me since the day I got that blue envelope with news of my husband's death, I didn't hesitate for a single second before answering.

"I want to live," I said.

And that was the exact moment when my life really started.

****

"Elizabeth sent for you," Ludovic said. I had been staring into space, lost in the memories of the day I'd met him and his sister. A cautious smile bloomed on his otherworldly, golden face, and tight black ringlets clouded his eyes. He swiped them away so quickly that his hand wasn't more than a blurry shadow passing his forehead.

"Please tell her I will be right there."

Ludovic nodded and left.

I looked at the clock on the wall: it was early for the queen to call a meeting. As soon as I stood up, an idea sprang to mind. Elizabeth didn't like waiting, but I had to get it on paper before I forgot.

Tearing off the previous page of my diary, I leaned over the paper and traced the new opening line with the most ornate calligraphy I could muster:

"My name is Julia, and I am a witch."

Chapter 2

Iulia

March 1946

The woman who had captured me in the forest disappeared in a puff of smoke.

Where she had stood, a small raven fluttered and glided up above the trees, disappearing into the dark, moonless night.

I stifled a cry, unwilling to believe what my eyes had just seen: an impossibly strong woman who could turn into a raven and fly away. What kind of creature was that, and why was it roaming Saint Emery's cemetery at night?

The man in front of me shook his head with apprehension. His icy hand released my wrist and grasped my hand instead, with equal tenacity.

"Please, let me go," I pleaded, staring into his eyes with fear. In response, he just looked away—there was guilt in the way he ignored me, but clearly a guilt he wasn't going to acknowledge. "What do you want from me?" I whimpered.

"Honestly? I want you and your kind to let us live in peace. That's what I want," he answered cryptically. "But my sister thinks otherwise."

"Leave you in peace?" I blinked, unable to understand. "Sir, look at me!" I pointed to my patched brown skirt. "Forgive me, but what kind of threat could someone like me pose to a man like you?"

He was tall and well-built, and his smooth complexion and silky fingers suggested a life of comfort and privilege, away from the fields and the lung-wrecking factories where most inhabitants of Saint Emery, including me, worked their days away.

He watched me closely, again pausing for a second too long on my neck, and his eyes softened as he noted how unintimidating I looked.

"Please, have mercy," I said once more, but he ignored my request and kept walking.

We reached the train station, where he bought two tickets to Emberbury, a middle-sized town west of Boston.

"Do you have a family?" he asked. "An elderly mother to care for? Children waiting at home?"

I shook my head, wiping off my tears discreetly as we got on the train. I tried not to think of loneliness as a foe but a friendly creature living inside my chest: as long as I fed it often enough, it would take care of me and protect me from the outside world. Sometimes it showed its teeth, but it happened only sporadically.

"Good." He seemed satisfied with the answer. "What's your name?"

"Julia. Julia Reighton."

He nodded and remained silent, tapping with long fingers on the armrest.

"May I know yours?" I said in a low voice.

The man looked around, making sure we were alone in the carriage. "I'm concerned what you might do with that information."

His response made me burst into laughter. It was a bitter, possibly hysterical laugh, appropriate for the irrationality of the situation. I thought I was about to go insane. "Yes. Because, that way, I could put your name in a jar and sell your soul to the devil, isn't that so?"

Judging by the way he looked at me, I might have read his mind. I didn't really blame him, after seeing a woman disappear into a mist.

"Where did you get that pendant?" he asked, pointing at my silver necklace. It was shaped like an upside-down tree with several branches, and each of them held a different object: a key, a moon, a bird and a snake. Even though I didn't know its meaning, I wore it because it reminded me of Gabriel.

"It was my late husband's," I answered, holding the pendant in my hand. I had never seen my husband wearing it, but nevertheless, that trinket had become my anchor, my last connection to him in the dark, postwar days.

"That's an interesting piece of jewelry for your husband to keep," he commented in a softer voice. His face was framed by a mane of black curls and nicely groomed—if outdated—sideburns. "Was he Italian?" he asked with curiosity.

Feeling suddenly brave, I echoed his previous apology, "I'm concerned what you might use that information for."

"I see. You can call me Ludovic," he said tautly.

I felt slightly better after that small victory. "No, he wasn't Italian," I said, "but he died near Bari. This was among the personal effects I received after his death."

"Most interesting indeed," he said, motioning as if to touch it but recoiling at the last moment. "Do you know what it means?"

"It means he's dead, and I'm on my own now," I answered, and closed with my eyes.

***

"Witches stink."

A caramel-skinned lady greeted us grimly on our arrival. I had pretended to sleep during the train ride, spying on my captor, Ludovic, with half-closed eyes. I had hoped for him to stand up and give me an opportunity to escape, but he had just sat there like a wax figure. Finally, Emberbury Park Station had been announced and we had got off.

An hour before dawn, Ludovic had brought me through a series of underground galleries beneath an abandoned cemetery into a clandestine dwelling he had matter-of-factly called a vampire nest.

"A… what?" I had asked in shock, but he had ignored the question and told me to get ready to meet their ruler. Shortly afterward, a middle-aged and very regal-looking lady called Elizabeth Swamp stood in front of me, calling me a witch.

"What am I supposed to do with her?" she asked, sniffing me once again with disgust. The queen was sitting in a red velvet armchair, wearing a skirt with at least three petticoats and white gloves which contrasted against her bronze forearms. As she spoke, the tiny blond girl from the graveyard made her appearance and sat down next to her.

"The smell is so overpowering that we're going to have to vacate the premises if she stays here for too long," Elizabeth complained.

"Do you find her tempting?" the girl—Francesca—asked. She was the harpy who thought killing a grieving widow was a wonderfully magnanimous gesture.

Elizabeth snorted. "Did you fall on your nose and injure it, Francesca? How could a stinky witch be appealing to a vampire?"

That word again.

"That's what I thought," the tiny blonde girl answered. "Nobody would want to bite her, and that makes her a great candidate to take care of our daytime affairs. She could serve us for a long time. Work for us, without being a constant warm blooded temptation. Let's use her to take care of all those annoying tasks which must be tackled from dawn to dusk." Francesca glanced at me. "You said you weren't interested in dying, didn't you?"

I didn't answer, mostly because I had been in shock for the best part of the night and my lips were sealed by sheer dread.

"That's the most absurd proposal I have ever heard," the queen answered. "A witch! In our house!"

But despite her dismay, less than two hours later, Elizabeth Swamp assigned me a room in the catacombs.

And that was how I became the lowliest member of Emberbury's vampire clan in a place called The Cloister.

***

Emberbury, April 1946

A man's screams woke me.

I had been living with the vampires for one month, and by then, I knew my way around the catacombs quite well. Silently, I tiptoed all the way to the large room where I had met the vampire queen on my arrival. The door was half open, and I spied a small group of vampires congregated around a man, who lay on the floor in a fetal position, covering his head with his arms.

"How long have you been spying on us?" Elizabeth asked him.

The man whined and curled up even tighter.

"I just wanted to be one of you," he whined. "I promise I didn't have any ill intentions."

Elizabeth snorted. "I'm sorry to inform you that I cannot grant you such a wish. There's only one sentence for those who meddle with our affairs uncalled. And do you know what it is… *Ralph*? Was it Ralph?"

The man sobbed. "Please, have mercy. I swear, I didn't tell anyone."

"He's been lingering near The Cloister for months. At first, we didn't attach much importance to his frequent presence around the graveyard grounds at night, but this evening I caught him trying to get in," a red-haired vampire said. She approached the moaning man and kicked him in the ribs with visible enjoyment. "We had a pleasant conversation about it earlier, didn't we, Ralph?"

"Did you try to make him forget, Lillian?" Elizabeth said sternly. "You know I'm not a supporter of gratuitous slaughter."

"Oh, of course I tried the oblivion. But his memories seem to go too far back. It's a hopeless case. I suggest we end his suffering now."

"And you will kindly volunteer to do it, won't you, Lillian?" Ludovic said. He had been standing in a corner with his arms crossed in front of his chest.

"Unless you want to, dear Ludovic." Lillian smiled, showing her fangs clearly. She was surprisingly tall, and her nose was covered in freckles, which together with her pale skin, gave her the appearance of a stout but oddly anemic farmer-girl.

Ludovic shook his head and withdrew back to the corner. Elizabeth gathered her skirt and exhaled with impatience.

"I'm retiring now. I'm hungry, but I don't like the taste of moles. Make sure you dispose of the human spy properly, Lillian."

The queen moved to leave and I looked around, frantically searching for a place to hide. Finally, I crouched behind a statue which stood behind a turn of the dark corridor. I knew Elizabeth's chambers were in the opposite direction, and hopefully, she would head there. The queen exited the room and turned right, walking away from my hiding spot. She didn't notice me. When she disappeared, I let out a deep breath and said a brief prayer of thanks.

The screams coming from the room became intolerable. I crept back to my prying place and glanced at the scene going on in the conference hall.

If I had still doubted the existence of

vampires, all my hesitations dissipated in that very moment.

Lillian was literally tearing the spy into pieces. She had ripped off his clothes, and her fangs tore whole chunks of naked flesh mercilessly. Blood dripped down her chin as she sucked at his throat, legs and arms, cackling and dancing around him in a macabre ballet. All that time, she took good care of keeping him conscious. As soon as he started to faint, she slapped him and woke him up again.

"Enough, Lillian!" Ludovic shouted, stepping in heatedly. "Just drain him already, will you? You made your point."

"Let me enjoy my toy, will you? It's not every day that I get Elizabeth's permission to slay a mortal at leisure."

Ludovic growled and pushed Lillian away. He crouched next to the man and, with a swift move of his hand, broke his neck. I heard a dry crack and the man's whines stopped abruptly as life finally left his body. Horrified as I was, I couldn't help but let out a hushed sigh of relief.

Lillian snarled and kicked the bloody mass on the floor with hardly contained anger.

"You!" She hissed, looking at Ludovic through half-closed eyes. "He was mine to kill! Mine!"

Ludovic ignored her and strolled toward the door. The furious red-haired vampire perched on the neck of her lifeless victim and ripped off the head with frustration. The sound of bones and muscle tearing was nothing short of blood-curdling.

"Elizabeth gave him to me!" she shrieked, sucking on the headless body.

My stomach turned, and I felt the urge to throw up. Unfortunately, there was no time for that: Ludovic was about to exit the room. If I didn't flee fast enough, he would find me snooping. I scanned the halls for the quickest route of escape. Keeping my back against the damp stone walls, I sneaked into the corridor which led back to my bedroom.

"Julia, you can go back to bed now and stop spreading your stench all over the hallways," Elizabeth said.

She had been standing in the darkness all that time. Instead of continuing to her chambers, she had remained to listen.

And now she was aware that I had seen everything.

"I'm glad you were here tonight," she said with a pearly white smile, "because now you know what happens to those who betray us."

***

Emberbury, May 1946

The creatures called their underground dwelling *The Cloister*, and I found the name quite fitting. Not only because of the Gothic colonnades carved in the reddish stone of the walls; but also because of the monastic life I had been condemned to in exchange for staying alive.

It was the life of a cloistered nun, just not an ordinary one: a nun whose mission was to serve the seven remaining vampires of Emberbury in the utmost secrecy. They weren't able to walk outside in the sun, and that made me useful in their eyes.

The scent of my blood was utterly revolting to most of them. Elizabeth said I stank of rotten cilantro, and Francesca simply called it *witch smell.* Anyhow, that seemed to keep their fangs away from my throat, which was good news for me.

Gabriel's pendant often attracted their fascinated stares. Almost every day, I caught a vampire staring at the silver amulet around my neck. They eyed it as though it were the devil itself, rarely commented, and never tried to touch it. I suspected there must be a link between my amulet and their belief that I was a witch.

Despite having seen what these human-looking creatures were capable of, the word *vampire* was still a hard one to swallow. In my head, I usually called them *night creatures* and other similar euphemisms; but they used the term with ease, like it didn't evoke horrific images of gory murder and bloodshed.

Putting aside the scene with Lillian and the spy, those seven creatures behaved with surprising civility in my presence. Altogether, they demonstrated better manners than most ordinary people I had met under the sun.

It took me a couple of months, but I ended up accepting my new life. After all, it wasn't much worse than working in a factory sunrise-to-sunset and returning each night to a room that smelled of mildew and felt full of echoes and memories of departed loved ones.

The vampires never tried too hard to keep me captive. It must have been apparent that I had nowhere better to go. Knowing what happened to those who got on their wrong side, I had absolutely no intention of becoming their next human toy. And certainly Elizabeth counted on that.

After a while, the queen stopped gagging when she saw me and started to give me simple tasks to complete for her:

Go to the bank.

Buy me this from the market.

Bring a parcel to this address.

Suddenly, I was allowed to roam the city freely again. The job was easy, and they paid me for it. They also fed me properly, and there was no mention of fangs, blood, or slaughtering anymore. Sometimes, a raven hovered over my head as I carried out my errands, and I wondered whether it was one of them patrolling, watching my moves. But many days they just trusted me to go back of my own accord.

I always did.

Every night, one of the vampires knocked on my door and invited me to join them in the library or in the music room.

Every single time, I declined, remembering what they were.

By the end of the summer, even those qualms started to soften and fade. The vampires left me alone as long as I did what they asked me to. They were courteous, if distant.

I even started thinking that maybe, *just maybe*, being abducted by a vampire clan had been a blessing in disguise.

I even forgot a little about Gabriel's empty tomb and a couple of times I failed to feed the hungry, dark void inside my heart.

They say that sleeping dogs must be allowed to lie; and following the same logic, corpses were best left to rest in peace for eternity. But, for some reason, I couldn't resist the urge to raise the ghost which was haunting me.

It shouldn't have come as a surprise that, in between raising ghosts and waltzing with death, I ended up falling in love with an undead.

Chapter 3

Iulia

Emberbury, August 1946

The door to my room opened, and Ludovic came in, formal as usual, but carrying an unexpected gift.

"The Dark Arts of Magic, by Catalina Kodrinova," he recited ceremoniously, handing me a worn and tattered book. It looked old and filthy, though not exactly antique.

"What is this?" I asked, holding the musty volume with just two fingers and studying the golden-skinned vampire in front of me.

Ludovic had taken to paying me a brief visit every other day—perhaps to make sure nobody had devoured me yet. At first, our exchanges had been stiff; but slowly, they had become friendlier. As much as I refused to acknowledge it, I had come to eagerly await his arrival. Maybe I was just lonely, or perhaps there was something about him which stirred up the longing for darkness inside me.

"I thought you might find this read interesting. It was in our library, though I don't know how it ended up there."

"A book of spells?" I asked, arching my eyebrows in surprise. "I've never cast a spell in my life."

He raised an eyebrow skeptically. "Then it might be time you started," he said in all seriousness. "Isn't that what you witches do? Turn people into toads? Make it rain when there's a draught?"

I wondered whether he really believed that or he was just trying to be funny—in a vampire way.

"Sounds exciting, but… I'm not much of a spellcaster."

Since my arrival at The Cloister, I had let them believe that I was a witch who had forgotten how to do magic. After all, it had been their idea, not mine. Provided that it kept me alive and fed, I didn't really mind playing along with their game.

The vampire snatched the book from my hands and opened it randomly, taking a seat on the chair next to me.

"It can't be so hard," he said, thumbing through the yellowed pages. "Looks just like a cookbook to me."

Ludovic pointed at an arbitrary paragraph and started to read aloud:

"In order to find a lost familiar, mix a whole pot of boiled mice ear mites with two ounces of golden meteorite powder and stir until dawn under a new moon. Bury the concoction in a king's stables and watch your wishes come true within five days."

I snorted, and his lips curled up in an apologetic smile. "I could get you the ear mites," he muttered with a shrug.

He can be sweet sometimes, was my first thought.

He's a vampire, was the next one, and I sighed involuntarily, remembering how he had snapped the spy's neck without even flinching.

"Easier to find ear mites than chocolate in postwar times, I'd bet," I said. "You know what? I think I'll read it. I've seen harder recipes in French cookbooks."

"Are you familiar with French cookbooks?" he asked, jerking his head back with astonishment.

"Well, at least more than most people." I shrugged. "My father was a baker, and I used to be his helper."

"Was he? How fascinating. I'd really like to hear about that," he said, leaning in my direction. "I've often wondered what innovations came to light in the culinary world in the last couple of centuries."

"Why would a vampire be interested in food? I thought you ate only one thing."

"You would be surprised, but most vampires

used to lead conventional, boring lives before becoming—" he paused, measuring his words, "—all pale and frightening. And I still like sweets, anyway."

"Oh, really?" I said with disbelief. "What's a *familiar*, anyway?" I asked, remembering the spell he had just read, "Is it like a family member?"

"As far as I know, a familiar is usually part of a witch's family, yes. But not a human one."

"Aha. Well, come to think of it… I might have a way to put that invocation to use…"
Finding Gabriel.

"I'm not sure the spell would work with deceased people," he said cautiously, correctly guessing what I was thinking about. "Or with people, at all. Familiars are spirits with an animal form."

"Well, if the book is called The *Dark* Arts of Magic, it should be able to accomplish eerie things, shouldn't it? I can't think of anything darker than working with dead people."

His eyes smiled slightly, and I couldn't help but smile back at his charming response.

"Very well." He nodded. "Let's reach a compromise."

"What kind of compromise?" I asked with intrigue as he stood up. He offered me a hand to shake and I took it. It was cold, but his touch was pleasant, almost electric.

"You stop hiding here all by yourself and join us in the library," he said, guiding me out of the room like we were about to dance, "and, in exchange, I will find a whole pot of boiled mice ear mites for you. Then you just have to find some golden meteorite powder, and I daresay Elizabeth owns at least one stable where you could bury the concoction. She's the closest thing to a king you will find in godforsaken Emberbury."

***

That summer night, I joined the vampires in the library for the first evening since my arrival in early spring.

The Cloister's archives were an underground wonder comparable to a well-stocked public library, only more sophisticated and quiet. Rows and rows of books extended as far as the eye could see. The space was cathedral-shaped and reached a considerable height above the floor. I wondered whether they also had cookbooks, or chemistry books: I had always found both fascinating and oddly similar; but never had the funds to buy any.

Francesca, my captor-savior, was also there, sitting on a comfortable-looking couch in a pearly white dress suitable for a bride—a vampire bride who should have been dead for at least a century.

"So, you finally came out of your den," she pointed out casually, setting aside an obscure-looking volume on music theory.

I frowned, refusing to respond to such

provocation. It wasn't like I had burrowed myself into that *den* of my own accord. Francesca's first impression had had a lot to do with it.

"Why don't you sit next to me?" Francesca said, patting a vacant spot by her side on the couch. "I like to feel a mortal's warmth. It feels so cozy."

Yes, excellent. That was so inviting. As much as I tried to hide it, I still resented her for trying to sink her fangs into my neck that first night in the forest.

"I'd rather have my own chair, but thanks."

I slumped into the furthest seat I could find and opened *The Dark Arts of Magic* at the first page. Maybe sharing a room with a woman who had tried to kill me wasn't such a good idea, after all. At least the grimoire was large enough and created a nice barrier against unpredictable Francesca.

"I see you are still cross with me," she stated in a sweet voice.

"Wouldn't you be, if you were in my place?"

She let her book fall into her lap and gave me a magnified blink. "You were talking to an empty grave. You said yourself you wanted to die. Why should I be sorry for fulfilling your wishes?"

"How did you know my husband's tomb was empty?" I asked, ignoring the last part of her speech.

Francesca leaned back on the couch. "We can sense that."

Yes, Gabriel's name had been engraved on the Reighton mausoleum, but his body had never made it back home. I had been left alone with just a letter from the army, a pendant I'd never seen before and a hollow grave to cry on.

"He died in Italy," I said, feeling a compelling need to empty my soul and finish what I had been trying to do that night at the graveyard.

"So his remains stayed there?" she asked with interest, changing seats to be closer to me.

"I suppose," I said slowly. Ludovic approached us and seated himself in the armchair right next to mine. Both vampires leaned toward me with interest, and I faltered for a second before continuing. "They never found him, really. There was an explosion, and many soldiers died on that day. They found Gabriel's name tag in the area and his helmet. Later, a surviving sergeant contacted me and gave me the few personal effects he had left at the barracks, including this pendant." I pressed the chain in my palm, feeling its reassuring presence.

"So his body was never found, technically."

"Many bodies weren't found," I said tiredly. "But where else could he be?"

"And you had never seen that pendant before?" Francesca waved toward my tree-shaped silver pendant, careful not to touch it.

"I don't really understand the relationship between a piece of jewelry and my husband's disappearance."

I squirmed in my seat and the siblings gave each other a meaningful look.

"Maybe there is a link, and maybe there's

not," Francesca said deliberately, staring mysteriously into her brother's eyes. "Don't you find it strange that you never saw that thing before?"

I shrugged. "We were married for a couple of weeks before he left, and he died many months later. You will understand there was much I didn't have time to learn about him."

"I think you should definitely research the matter a bit deeper. Maybe visit Italy. See for yourself," Francesca said matter-of-factly, and I couldn't help but sneer at her ingenuity.

"And how am I supposed to do that? Should I just turn into a raven and fly across the ocean?"

"We might be able to help," Francesca said, taking Ludovic's hand in hers.

"The last time you tried to help me, you almost drained all the blood in my veins, so no thank you," I said, wrinkling my nose.

The way she smiled back, it was clear that she felt no remorse whatsoever.

"We know someone in Italy," Ludovic said, speaking for the first time. "We could ask her to go and have a look, if you know approximately where it happened."

"And why would you do that?" I asked, crossing my arms over the still open witchcraft book.

"To help you find closure," he said, nodding sympathetically.

***

The Dark Arts of Magic by Catalina Kodrinova proved to be a thought-provoking yet baffling read.

From spells to turn yourself into a bat and spy on your enemies, to potions able to cause a prince to fall in love with you hopelessly, Kodrinova had just about covered anything a budding witch of the Middle Ages might have required to cater to a very colorful clientele—and herself.

Such a shame that most of the ingredients were simply impossible to find in the current era.

I lay on my bed and browsed the grimoire for the easiest spell of all, searching for one with materials I might be able to source in modern day Emberbury. After a brief search, I spotted one titled *"Green Luminescence."*

Not my favorite color, but it seemed easy enough.

"This spell will be valuable to light underground passages and coves. Use it sparingly, for it can damage the sorcerer's vision and internal organs. Once in a blue moon, it can be valuable to scald a rival's hands. Never keep the glow burning for longer periods."

I doubted anything would start to glow at all,

so I wasn't too concerned about damaging my vision or internal organs due to excessive use of magic. As a bonus, the only ingredients needed were a candle and a stone, and I knew where to get both.

I would just pretend it was a cookbook, just like Ludovic had suggested.

The next evening, I settled at my bureau desk with the open spell book, a rock from Saint Anne's cemetery and a brand new white candle. I read the magic words and proceeded as directed. To finish the spell, I placed the stone over the candle flame and whispered the magic words, "*Viridi Lux*," then waited for my enchanted torch.

I didn't believe anything would happen.

But then, a soft green glow enveloped the stone, and the candlelight extinguished with a sound resembling a soft sigh.

The stone was glowing!

Amazed, I took the rock in both hands, feeling a jolt when it stung my skin. With the candle snuffed, darkness fell over the room, and the only source of radiance was the small object shining on my palms. Staring at it in awe, I tried to touch it again. This time, it burned my fingers just a little. My eyes teared up when I stared at the green light directly, so I turned my head to the side. The glow might be gentle, but there was definitely something caustic about it: something dangerous.

The greenish luminescence, with its corroding touch, reminded me of the story of another woman who had spent her life staring at glowing deadly things, up to her very last day. A woman I had first read about while waiting for baguette dough to rise.

"Is that magic?" I had often asked my father with wide eyes, as the miracle of yeast turned flour into bread.

"Not magic, just science," he had answered invariably, implying science was something much less remarkable. He was angry at science because it hadn't been able to save my mother and my little brother.

Since an early age, whenever he allowed me to help in the bakery, I had volunteered to mix and measure batter ingredients. Cakes and icings were my favorites, because they required extreme precision. While other girls dreamed of cradling babies, I had fantasized about *making science*, whatever that was. In my imagination, I combined secret ingredients and found a cure for all the world's ailments. As I blended royal icing for a noble wedding cake or a rich industrialist's birthday, the bowl turned into an Erlenmeyer flask, full to the brim with miraculous compounds which would save all children of the universe from suffering.

At the age of eleven, I read on the front page of my father's newspaper a headline about a woman named Marie Curie. The article was about the death of a respectable lady, pictured below in black-and-white, and they called her *a scientist*. I stole the paper and read the piece sneakily, locked in the storage room of the bakery, amazed to find out that scientist was a career. Not only that, female scientists actually existed outside my childish imaginings.

From then on, I told myself I would become like her. I would have my own laboratory, and I'd make things glow, explode, appear and disappear.

But of course, going to university was out of reach for the daughter of a small-town baker who didn't even have a business of his own. My father was just an employee, and when the bakery closed, he couldn't even manage to send me to a proper baking school, let alone a university. I ended up standing behind the assembly lines, just like the rest of my schoolmates, and dreaming of all the findings I would never discover.

That night in The Cloister, holding a glowing stone in my hand, I felt like my dream had just come true. I might not be a scientist like Marie Curie, but I could become an alchemist. A magician.

"Is this how it felt, Mrs. Curie?" I asked her ghost, in case she could hear me. "Discovering something magical? Gazing at something nobody had seen before?"

The sound of a rustling cloak interrupted my daydream, and I turned around to find Ludovic staring at the shining stone.

"Who is Mrs. Curie?" he asked.

"A woman who made rocks glow," I answered dreamily. "Only she didn't even need magic for it,"

I doubted Ludovic had ever heard about her, isolated in his underground catacomb as he was.

"I know who she was," he said, surprising me, "I just didn't expect you to."

I rolled my eyes at his comment, and he smiled. Then he reached out to touch the rock, but his hand flew back swiftly, and he flinched with visible surprise.

"It stings, yes," I said, shrugging in apology.

"How did you manage to do it?" he asked, pointing at the otherworldly greenish light over the desk.

"I don't know," I answered in awe, "I just followed the instructions in the grimoire. You said it was like a cookbook, so I treated it as such: this was the only recipe I had all the ingredients for. I didn't think it would work but… it did."

"So, the spells are real," he said with admiration, brushing his fingers against my arm. This time he was careful to avoid the treacherous piece of gravel.

"They are," I whispered.

"Absolutely mesmerizing," he muttered in amazement. When I followed his gaze and found it on my hands, I wasn't really sure whether his admiration was directed to the magic object or the newly minted sorceress.

***

After that magical night when I cast my first spell, I spent many hours with my nose in Kodrinova's grimoire, taking notes and seeking useful skills to learn.

Soon I realized that, if I was able to make an ordinary rock glow, I might also have the power to achieve much greater things.

Like finding out what happened to Gabriel.

Or making world-changing discoveries.

I would welcome whatever happened first.

But so far, the *Luminescent Glow* seemed to be the only incantation which didn't include ingredients as far-fetched as one-legged bats' teeth or South Polynesian double black pearls.

The ingredient part was still absolutely frustrating.

A grandfather clock chimed midnight in the distance. I had been up reading for hours, and despite my tiredness, sleep evaded me.

The vampires must be out and about, but nobody had forbidden me to roam around The Cloister at will. I decided to have a walk and stretch my legs: maybe that would help make me a bit drowsier.

As I paced the silent halls, I remembered the night when Lillian had tortured a man in front of my eyes. Gloomily, I wondered how I had become so indifferent to the nature of the creatures I shared a roof with. Had I turned into a modern, female version of Dracula's Renfield? What happened to the little girl who had dreamed of saving lives and curing sick children?

The answer was simple: she had been crushed by poverty, war and hunger. She had been trampled by an outside world so ruthless that it was worse than living with a clan of potential slaughterers beneath a graveyard.

At least it was a pretty graveyard, unlike the homes I had lived in up to then.

Marching noiselessly down a corridor, I gaped at the stone walls, covered in artistic oil paintings and tapestries. Some statues seemed to be made of pure gold. Only the lack of windows and natural light gave away the unusual nature of The Cloister's inhabitants.

One of the doors was ajar. I approached it curiously and pushed the handle.

I found myself at the entrance of an elegantly decorated nook, with a desk just like mine. Sitting at the table was Ludovic, with his head buried in a gigantic map of Europe. The papers poured over the sides of the table and extended over half of the room like a carpet.

The floor was covered in old newspapers, some open, some not. A quick look at the headlines confirmed my suspicion that all of them were connected to battles fought in the south of Italy from 1944 to 1945.

"Please, do come in," Ludovic said, looking

surprised by the intrusion, but clearly not upset. He marked a spot on the map with a polished gem and stood up to receive me. "I didn't expect to find you awake at this hour. But it's nice you came. I was just researching your husband's case."

The word *husband* sounded peculiar when he pronounced it. It might have been his odd accent, or maybe, just maybe, there was a slightly bitter tinge in his voice.

The room was singularly chilly, and I pulled at the sides of my thin cardigan in a vain attempt to fight the frosty draft coming from the slit under the door.

"You must be cold," he said, noticing my discomfort and taking off his cloak. He wrapped the soft garment around my shoulders, and his bergamot scent swathed me.

"Better," he said, nodding with satisfaction. "Sorry about the draft."

I crouched and flipped through the dozens of maps and newspapers on the floor.

"I see you were serious about helping me find Gabriel," I said with amazement. It was remarkable that he had conducted all this research on his own and didn't even find it worth mentioning. "Why are you doing this?"

"Because otherwise, you will always wonder," he said, measuring his words. "You won't be able to truly start anew until you close that chapter of your life."

Closing my eyes, I nodded, astonished he understood me so well. As much as I wanted to move on, the uncertainty of whatever had happened to Gabriel made it hard to concentrate on new things, be it work, or magic, or…

Ludovic sat on his heels next to me and started to put the papers in an orderly pile, leaving his eyes locked on mine.

"Thank you," I whispered, draping myself tighter in the smooth cloak. That made me envision his arms embracing me, and I blushed.

"It would be a pity to deprive the world of the first confectioner able to bake glowing cakes," he said with a fond smile.

"It was never my dream to become a confectioner, but thank you anyway," I answered, drawing forward in his direction, like the attraction of an invisible magnet.

"So what did you want to be?" His head was tilted, his gaze expectant.

"I thought I wanted to be a scientist, but maybe an alchemist would suit me better. Back then, I still didn't know about that possibility." I glanced at the many books on his shelves and wondered whether it would be possible to read them all in a human lifespan. Probably not.

"I like alchemists," he said warmly. "They turn everything into gold."

"And they can brew immortality elixirs," I added dreamily. *Not that he needed that.*

A knock on the door made us rise abruptly, watering down the enchantment of the moment. Francesca made her appearance, wearing a full skirt that was wider than the doorframe; a short Victorian cape and bonnet made her look like a lost time traveler.

"Brother," she said, "let's go. You must be thirsty. I know I am."

Ludovic smiled weakly and took my hand, helping me to stand up with gallantry. "Let me see Julia to her room first," he said.

We walked in silence, and he bowed farewell. Once he left, I watched the door and pondered mindlessly about whose neck his lips might be sinking into. For a fleeting second, I wished it were mine. Shaking my head, I dismissed such ghastly fantasies with a frustrated moan.

I fell asleep much later, right after the sound of steps filled the halls once again. The last thing I heard before I closed my eyes was the sound of both siblings laughing quietly as they dashed past my door.

Chapter 4

Julia

Emberbury, October 1946

It was a chilly autumnal day in Emberbury, and I spent it doing some errands and enjoying my new means of travel.

Elizabeth had suggested I should buy myself a bicycle, and I had gladly obliged. That day, I was feeling glorious, riding my brand-new red *porteur* for the first time. The bike had a beautiful steel rack on the front and a large, handy basket to carry groceries and parcels, both very convenient for my job. The sky was steel-gray, threatening rain, and I tried to avoid possibly lethal puddles. Smoky chimneys and impending storms perfumed the sharp fall air. I still hadn't adjusted to the city and I often missed my home village, Saint Emery, and its peaceful roads. But Emberbury had a charm of its own, on top of the hundreds of stores and available products to be bought, if one happened to have the money, which I suddenly had for the first time in my life.

Ludovic had asked me to get hold of any newspapers from the summer 1944. He had mentioned a bookstore in downtown Emberbury owned by two twin brothers. They were known for their uncanny ability to find just about any publication, old or new, as long as there was still one printed copy in the whole world.

I grabbed a sandwich from a cart by the street and asked the seller for directions. The bookstore wasn't easy to find, despite its considerable size. It was late afternoon when I finally spotted the narrow sign over the entrance, with the name *Rare Books Brothers Sheen* in delicate golden lettering. The shop had many windows, but they were all closed and darkened with half-drawn blinds, possibly to avoid the sun from damaging the vintage books they carried.

There were two identical men sitting at the counter, both sporting mousy chestnut hair sleekly styled back with jelly, dusty ties and ratty brown jackets which had obviously seen better days. They must be the Sheen brothers.

One of them marked a page in his book and stood up to greet me. "Good morning, Miss, how can I help you?"

Meanwhile, the other one kept reading, completely oblivious to my presence. I noticed the counter was a carved wooden work of art in itself, with a countertop made of glass. Under it, the Sheens had displayed a selection of antique jewels and ornaments. The objects were diverse, ranging from a golden cornucopia to a tiny bronze Venus. There were also a few ancient-looking coffrets, which might have contained just about anything—maybe even some golden meteorite powder to use in a spell. All the items had price tags, which must mean they were for sale.

"I'm looking for old newspapers," I said to the bookseller, "namely, those published during the summer of 1944. I'm interested in every piece of news you can find about battles fought around Bari, Italy."

Mr. Sheen examined me with squinting eyes, taking in my head-to-toe dark clothes, and nodded.

"I see," he said, "I'm not sure I have anything here, but I might be able to get them for you, if you are willing to wait for a couple of weeks."

"Time is not a problem," I said.

Gabriel wasn't going anywhere, as far as I knew.

"Let me make a phone call and please have a look at our book selection while you wait," he said, waving at the alluring heaps of old-smelling volumes around us. "If you need anything, you can ask Ed." He pointed at the reading man, who didn't even lift his head to acknowledge the observation. "I'm Stan, by the way."

Stan shook my hand and disappeared

through a door behind the counter.

The Sheens had done a good job collecting books from the four winds. They even had foreign publications on the shelves: old Greek and Latin titles and encyclopedias so thick that they would have sufficed to heat a large family home by burning them one volume at a time during the coldest days of winter.

Thinking of book burning suddenly reminded me of witchcraft treaties. If there was a bookstore in Emberbury which carried any of those, it had to be *Rare Books Brothers Sheen*. Maybe I'd be lucky enough to find something analogous to my everyday staple, *The Dark Arts of Magic*. And it would hopefully use easier-to-find spell ingredients.

I walked past two aisles labeled *Ancient History* and *Mystery Novels*, quickly scanning each of the labels on the tall wooden shelves. Soon, I realized there was no such thing as a dedicated section for witchcraft books.

"What are you searching for?"

To my utter surprise, Ed Sheen had lifted his binoculars off the page and was standing next to me, his arms crossed and an outright exasperated look in his face.

"Do you have anything by Catalina Kodrinova?" I asked hesitantly.

If he didn't, at least he wouldn't recognize the genre, saving me a great deal of awkwardness.

One of Ed's eyelids blinked several times

involuntarily. Then, he turned around and started to walk clumsily towards a corner of the store. Finally, he crouched in front of a small cupboard at floor level and opened it for me.

"Have a look here. I'd bet these titles may suit your liking."

There was an almost invisible metallic sign screwed to the inside of the doors, which conveniently read "*Occultism*". I squatted in front of the small closet next to Mr. Ed Sheen and had a quick look at the titles in there.

How to Conjure Ghosts and Banish Unwanted Spirits

The Ethical Necromancer's Guide
Love Filters and Potions
Memoirs of Viorel the Mage
Supernatural Tales of Faeries and Dragons

Despite the exorbitant prices, the need to own them all nearly overcame me.

"Um…" I hesitated, watching Ed Sheen twist his mouth in an almost impossible grimace. "Is there one you would particularly recommend?"

"Depends what for," Mr. Sheen growled back, running his fingers over the spines. He threw me a sidelong glance, and his eyes paused over my branched pendant. Raw garlic was clearly noticeable in his breath and the stench made me step back.

"Finding lost things?" I ventured, not wanting to give more information than necessary.

"Try this one," he said sullenly, picking up

the *Memoirs of Viorel the Mage* and thrusting it into my arms.

"Thank you," I said, rushing toward the counter to escape the man's vicinity, which was starting to become suffocating.

"Did you hear that?" Ed asked, spinning on the spot in a way no sober person would ever do.

"No, I'm sorry. I can't hear anything…"

"How can you not hear it?" Mr. Ed Sheen pounded on the top of a low bookcase, making a couple of books fall to the floor. "It's the specters screaming. They do that to welcome new company," he snarled like a wild animal, and I gasped in horror when his index finger pointed directly at me. "It's you! You!"

That man was completely insane.

I needed to get out of that store immediately.

"You know what, keep the book. I'll come back some other day," I muttered, getting rid of the sorcery tome and recoiling toward the door.

Ed started to chase me, and I had to dodge the counter to avoid his grip. However, the man crashed against it, and the glass top slid sideways and shattered on the floor with a loud clatter.

"You sorceress! You vampire wench!"

"What are you talking about?" I cried, fumbling with the exit door, which had become mysteriously locked.

Ed Sheen grabbed my pendant and pulled at it violently, trying to tear it off.

"Leave me alone!" I shouted, hitting him on the head with my heavy handbag.

The man stumbled back, and his brother appeared from the back room, throwing his hands on his head with consternation.

"I'm so sorry, madam!" Stan Sheen gulped loudly, staring at the mess. "My brother can be quirky from time to time, but it's nothing dangerous, I promise!" Then, turning toward Ed, he scolded him like he was a little child, "Ed! Look what you did! Sit down and behave properly!"

"I really need to leave," I said, still using my bag as a shield in case Ed Sheen had a relapse. "It's getting dark."

"Please come back next week," Stan said in a begging tone, as he helped me with the stuck door. "Don't take Ed seriously. He reads too many Victorian horror books."

As I was about to leave, he got on his knees and started to pick up glass shards, shaking his head with disapproval. "I made some phone calls for you, madam. I'm getting something very special by mail. Come back in a couple of weeks, and I'm sure you'll be delighted with my findings."

I answered with a forced smile and jumped on my bicycle, rushing back to The Cloister like a bat out of hell.

***

As I rode my bicycle under the flickering streetlights, I missed an almost invisible puddle of oil and lost control of the front wheel. The handlebar twisted backwards and I fell off, hitting my hip against the hard cobblestones.

Muttering a swearword, I stood up and tried to lift up the bicycle. The frame was bent, and the front wheel had unfastened from the fork, ending up on the other side of the road. Everything was warped and scratched. Angrily, I hauled the bike and started to walk toward The Cloister.

A man approached me in the darkness. I didn't even have to look at him to know it was Ed Sheen. He wore an enormous wooden crucifix around his neck and thrust it on my face with a demented expression.

"Is that supposed to fix my bicycle?" I asked, turning away from him and accelerating my pace.

"Witch!" he shouted in a shaky voice and poked my chest with the cross. "Cast the evil eye off me, you creature of hell!"

"Are you insane? There's only one evil-looking pair of eyes here, and it's definitely not mine."

Even though his brother had said he was harmless, I was starting to doubt his word.

I realized there was no way I could get rid of Ed Sheen if I had to haul my hefty bicycle back to Saint Anne's. I would have to choose between leaving my most precious possession by the road or listening to a madman go on about specters, witches and whatnot, and possibly pounce on me in a fit of lunacy.

Moving quickly, I leaned the metal frame against a wall and said a swift goodbye. It was bound to be stolen before I returned.

After that, I ran. I didn't look back until Ed Sheen's delirious chants became just a faint echo in the mists of the night and the welcoming gates of Saint Anne appeared in the distance.

Chapter 5

Iulia

October 1946

That evening, when Ludovic knocked on my door as usual, I was lying barefoot on the bed, languidly reading Catalina Kodrinova's book and taking lazy notes in my diary.

"Come in," I sang, quickly sitting up and making an effort to look as poised as possible.

Ludovic sat down in the armchair and watched me intently. He had one hand behind his back and he was clearly hiding something.

"Is anything wrong?" he asked, tilting his head with interest.

"No, everything is fine." I sighed, setting the book aside. "That is, apart from the madman who accused me of giving him the evil eye and followed me with a crucifix the size of Greenland." I didn't feel like talking about Ed Sheen: I wished I could forget about him forever. "But never mind. I'd rather know what's behind your back."

His jaw tightened just slightly, and I added for good measure, "I'm alright, and that's what counts."

"Very well," he said with a frown. "You'll tell me when you're ready."

"Of course," I said, willing to leave those disturbing memories behind. Ed Sheen was inoffensive. His brother had said it, and I wanted to believe it.

"I hope you will. If there's a lunatic bothering you, I'd love to pay him a courtesy visit."

"It's fine. I can sort it out on my own, really."

The way he narrowed his eyes, he wasn't going to let it go so easily, so I tried to change the subject.

"What are you hiding?" I asked, pointing at whatever he was concealing.

A mysterious smile formed on his lips. "I brought you a little present," he said, handing me an ornate cardboard box.

"Again? Don't tell me it's another grimoire," I said, intrigued. The box was small and lacy and most definitely didn't contain a book.

"No," he grinned, helping me to open the rounded white flaps and extracting a delicious-looking piece of lemon cake.

I gasped in surprise. "Well, this is unexpected!" I admired the tiny work of art. I couldn't even remember the last time I had tasted anything sweet. "I always loved royal icing."

Ludovic smiled with satisfaction. "I always wanted to try it."

He magically produced a silver spoon from a pocket in his silk vest and I took it ceremoniously.

"To what do I owe the honor?"

"We have something to celebrate," he said, "but let's try the cake first and discuss business later, or else the frosting might melt."

"This icing looks like Lambeth piping. Extremely difficult to master. I tried my hand at it many times, but I never got it right. In my father's words—I always gave up too quickly." I hesitated, hovering over the white and yellow decorations with Ludovic's silver spoon. Exquisite sugar waves and flowers festooned the fluffy sponge. "It's almost a sin, sinking into such delicate frosting, don't you think?"

"Let me do it if you want. I have no problems with sinning," he winked, and I felt my cheeks flush, wondering whether I had heard that right.

Slowly, I handed him the spoon, and watched him intently as he scraped a tiny amount of snow-white icing and put it in his mouth, then closed his eyes with feigned delight.

"So… do you like it?" I asked, expectant.

He opened one eye.

Then the other one.

"Actually, no," he said with a wrinkled nose,

and grinned as he pushed the lacy box in my direction. "All yours."

I laughed ridiculously loud, and he just sat there, with his shiny black curls falling unruly to one side.

As I tried to take the spoon from his hand, our fingers brushed for a second. His touch was electric, and it made me flinch. When he finally released the handle, I was already backing off, and the spoon fell on the stone floor with a soft clinking.

We both bent down to pick it up at the same time. Our eyes locked, and our hands clashed again over the fallen piece of silverware. I leaned forward, and so did he.

Face to face, I remained completely still, with my forehead just an inch away from his.

We were so close that I could feel the cold radiating from his skin.

And then, time froze.

None of us stepped back, but neither did we dare cross the invisible boundary between us.

Closing my eyes, I imagined what would happen if I tried to shatter that invisible barrier. It seemed so easy. So enticing. Carried away, I placed a shy kiss on his lips. It was quick, slight. Just like a feather's touch. Not weightier than a butterfly's wings.

As soon as I realized what I had just done, I backed off with a soft gasp, taking one hand to my chest.

"I…" *I'm sorry*, I was about to say, but paused. Actually, I wasn't sorry. Just a bit shocked by my heedless reaction.

Ludovic's hands found my waist and he scooped me up, keeping his gaze locked on mine. My own audacity had startled me, and I fell into an unexpected quiver. But I wasn't frightened: I just didn't recognize this bold version of myself.

Leisurely, he sat me on the edge of the bed and ducked his head until we were face to face. His eyes were oddly blue and fiery, shining like pools of light.

"Why are you shaking?" he asked hoarsely, brushing the back of his hand against my cheek. "Are you afraid of me, Julia?"

"No. I'm not."

My voice was firm, and Ludovic answered with a soft grunt. Then, he let his lips find mine and paused. His touch was an unspoken question. I didn't have to think twice about my answer.

Nodding just slightly, I grasped his shirt with both hands and pulled him against me.

This second kiss wasn't soft, nor was it shy. It was intense, and urgent, and completely dizzying. It was cool and tasted of tangerines and bergamot. It was the way all kisses of my life should have been, if only I had known before.

Ludovic closed his eyes, but I kept mine half open, unwilling to miss the perfection of those long, dark eyelashes and the bounce of his spiraling curls as he swayed to an inaudible music. I kissed him back with fervor, as his hands locked behind me in an embrace of steel.

For a few seconds, all was right in the world.

When his sharp fangs started to tease the skin under my chin, they stirred the darkness which had always inhabited the bottom of my soul. They tickled and prickled my neck just slightly, arousing me so badly that I had to gasp for air to avoid drowning in my own desire. He heard my sigh and staggered back, a bewildered look tarnishing his unblinking eyes.

"That wasn't supposed to happen," he said, turning away from me. His glance fell on my pendant, and he exhaled loudly.

In one swift move, he picked up the fallen spoon, which still lay forgotten on the floor and wiped it off on the tails of his shirt. "We really shouldn't allow that cake to melt."

***

We stared at each other awkwardly, and I sprung back to my feet, rushing toward the desk. Looking at the luxurious gateau, I realized with sorrow that I wasn't hungry anymore. Not for cake, anyway. But I couldn't put out of my mind how he had clearly stated that kissing me had been a mistake.

"Have you managed to get hold of any meteorite powder?" Ludovic said. I winced at his failed attempt at normalcy, but I decided to play along. "Maybe made anything... burn? Explode?"

I set the cake aside and straightened my shirt, decided to pretend nothing had just occurred between us. If he could do it, so could I.

"In fact, I haven't, but this afternoon it would have come in handy."

"So, are you going to finish telling me what happened to you on the street?" He peered at me from beneath a thick curtain of black ringlets.

I crossed my arms. "You aren't going to do anything to him, are you?"

"Why would I have a reason to?" Ludovic answered, raising an eyebrow.

"I heard you have some rules here which don't allow you to kill people just like that, is that right?" I'd make sure before telling him, just in case he happened to be hungry. I really wanted to get those Italian newspapers from the Sheens, and that would be hard to achieve if he killed them.

He narrowed his eyes, but nodded. "That's right. Those are The Cloister's rules. We are not permitted to make new vampires or kill any humans unless they really deserve it. Did this person deserve it by any chance?"

I shook my head, feeling upset about his arrogant attitude. "Of course not." I had been an orphan or a widow for half of my life, so I was more than capable of taking care of myself. "I don't want to cause him any harm. He's just a bit… disturbed. He hears things which aren't really there and his brother treats him like a little child. Not really his fault."

"Okay, so who is this *he*, if I may ask? I'm starting to get lost here," Ludovic tapped nervously on the desk, and the spoon rattled against the hardwood surface.

I exhaled tiredly. "Just one of the Sheens, from the bookstore. He called me a witch, and a—" my face must have turned completely red by then, "—a *vampire wench*, whatever that means."

Ludovic frowned. "I wonder why he'd say that."

"I don't know. I suppose it was just a strange coincidence. His brother said he's obsessed with ghost stories. The man started to act weird when I asked him to show me the esoteric section, then, after I left the store, I noticed someone was following me. But you don't have to worry, because he didn't see me come in."

"So, if I understand correctly, he followed you here?" Ludovic's voice sounded more heated with each minute that passed, possibly because he thought I had compromised the secrecy of The Cloister.

"No, of course not. I ran away."

"You had to run away?" He sounded aghast.

"Look, you know what, just forget it, will

you? He's just a bit imbalanced and behaved in a slightly sinister way. But I got away from him, so there's nothing to worry about. *All. Is. Fine.*"

"I tend to worry when sinister individuals follow you to our secret hideout." At this point, his voice was definitely beyond the maximum volume allowed in polite conversation.

"He didn't follow me to The Cloister; are you listening at all?" I raised my tone, trying to fend off his sudden protectiveness. "And, come to think of it, he wasn't so sinister. Not more than any of you, anyway!"

The moment I said it, I regretted it.

Sadly, it was impossible to erase words once pronounced.

Ludovic leaned back and away from me, lowering his gaze to the floor.

"I'm sorry you feel that way," he murmured with a deep sigh, flexing his legs to stand up. "I wish I could prove you wrong. But I don't think I can."

"Wait!" He was about to leave, so I reached for his forearm. He pushed me away gently. "I shouldn't have said that."

"You were just frank." He raised his palm between us, and I stepped back.

"Ludovic," I said, standing in front of him and thinking hard of a way to make him stay. "You said we had something to celebrate, remember?"

"Oh, yes," he answered, without a trace of joy in his voice. "It's about this person I know in Italy.

She agreed to join us in the search for your husband."

***

After Ludovic left my room, I noticed a sealed envelope on the floor: it must have fallen out of his pocket when he stood up from the armchair. Maybe, if I brought it back to him, we'd have a chance to reconcile and finish the evening on better terms.

I put on my shoes and threw a woolen cardigan over my shoulders, then walked up toward his chambers, down the candlelit corridors.

When I knocked on his door, nobody answered. He wasn't in the library, either, nor in the music room. After searching practically everywhere, I assumed he must have gone out to hunt. Somehow defeated, I turned around and decided to slip the envelope under his door.

As I passed Francesca's bedroom, I heard Ludovic's voice break the sepulchral silence of the galleries. I couldn't make out what he was talking about, but he sounded agitated. Angry, even.

I should have bolted back to my room at that very moment, but curiosity had glued my feet to the stone floor. I hated myself for snooping again, but it was stronger than me.

"It's a terrible idea," Francesca was saying. Ludovic's boots echoed inside as he paced around the room with impatience. "I know it was me who told Julia to find out about her husband, but now I see it was a misstep. I regret it."

"Rosanna owes us a favor." His voice was shaky, like he could hardly contain his uneasiness.

"No," Francesca continued. "Mortals always bring trouble. You have to stop this immediately. What if she comes here and Elizabeth sees her?"

"But I just promised Julia. I can't go back on my word now."

"My dear brother, you'd better before it's too late."

"How can you speak like that? Wasn't it you who lectured me about seeing the goodness in others? You, who regretted the loss of Angela for centuries?"

"What does this have to do with me? With Angela?" Francesca snapped, sounding furious. "If you are so keen to please that witch, then make up a story. Tell her what she wants to hear. What difference will it make? Will you risk everything we have for a mortal? For a dead one! Whoever that Mr. Reighton is, he's not worth one of us risking banishment."

"But it's important to her."

"To her? Or to you?"

There was a silence, and the pacing stopped.

"I don't want her to go back to see the Sheens. They suspect something. If we ask Rosanna, everything will be done much quicker. It will be safer for everyone, too."

"I don't care about those Sheens, and I can think of many ways of getting rid of two weak little humans. There's nothing they can do to me anymore."

"Yes, but what about Julia? What if she goes back there, searching for answers? What if they follow her again?"

"Well, if that's what worries you the most…" her voice became sensual, like a siren's, "Entertain her, *fratello mio*. Divert her attention so she stops thinking about that. You have done it before, haven't you? Just help her put her mind to other things. She will soon forget that deceased husband of hers. It's not like you don't have enough free time." Francesca's voice became suddenly emotionless, and she added, "use your charms, Ludovic. I know you have many of those, my darling brother."

Steps approached the door, and I held my breath. When they started to talk again, it was in a voice too low for me to hear.

So that was it. That was why our kiss had been a mistake. He didn't really want me. He was just doing what his sister wanted. And now they were trying to fool me about Gabriel's case, too.

I was such a fool. How could I ever believe anyone in The Cloister cared about me or my troubles?

Biting my lips, I controlled the urge to crumple up the letter. The envelope was addressed to Mrs. Rosanna Bianchi from Rome, and the sender was Mr. Ludovic Belak, without a street name or number. Still holding it, I tiptoed back to my room, making sure nobody followed me. Then I locked myself in and cried over Gabriel's picture until I fell asleep.

Chapter 6

Iulia

November 1946

A couple of days after I overheard the conversation between Ludovic and Francesca, I found a shiny new bicycle waiting for me on the frosty grass of the graveyard. It was leaning against the angel mausoleum, and its frame was the same shade of cobalt blue as Ludovic's eyes by candlelight.

Even though I hadn't told him about my little bike accident, there was no doubt about who could have bought the new one. Obviously, after hearing Francesca's advice for him, I wasn't going to give any of the Belak siblings the pleasure of touching any present of theirs.

After that night, I made a habit out of locking the door behind me whenever I retired to my room.

Ludovic knocked every single night. When he realized I wasn't letting him in any time soon, he started to invite me to spend time in the library, together with the others. Sometimes he tried to convince me to listen to Francesca play the piano, which I used to love.

But invariably, my answer was no.

After a while, the message hit home, and he gave up. Worry and sorrow kept me up far into the wee hours of the morning, but I wasn't going to let him *entertain me*—like Francesca had put it—just so he could abort my mission of finding out about Gabriel's fate.

When I was a little girl, my father had told me I would never master wedding cake icing, let alone go to university, because I always gave up too quickly. Well, I was going to show him, and anyone willing to watch, that new Julia could bring her mission to term—or die trying.

I had nothing better to do with my life anyway.

One morning, I ventured into the library, hoping to find all the vampires resting in their chambers after their nightly excursions. I listened before coming in—the place seemed completely silent. I would just pick a light novel to read in the evening and run to the conference room to meet Elizabeth.

Unfortunately, those creatures were silent as the Sphinx and had a habit of reading in the dark, so I didn't see the one sitting on the couch until I entered, and he stood up to greet me.

"Mrs. Reighton!" It was Clarence, a tall

English vampire with salt and pepper hair and maroon eyes. "How are you? I hear you have been keeping to yourself lately. Are you well?"

"Better than ever," I growled, striding toward the fiction shelves. "I should hurry up. Elizabeth is waiting for me."

"Oh, don't worry about Elizabeth. She's been talking to Ludovic for the entire night. I doubt she's there yet."

Clarence took a seat again and waved for me to join him. I obeyed reluctantly, perching on the edge of the divan with my back completely straight. Clarence was always so pristine that I found his appearance slightly unsettling—surreal, even.

"Was there anything you wanted to talk about?" I asked. Obviously, there was.

"I have noticed you seem to be quite… anxious lately," he said tactfully.

"I live surrounded by creatures which usually populate horror stories and nightmares. I don't know whether tomorrow I will wake up alive or with fang bites on my neck. And even if I don't, I'm not so naïve to ignore where all of you go at night while I try to sleep. You will have to agree that this is not the best place for a human to relax, won't you?"

"So, you're worried about all the awful things we do?" his eyes were sympathetic as he leaned with interest towards me. "What if I told you it's not as bad as you think?"

"I saw what Lillian did to that spy," I

answered stubbornly.

"You would be surprised, but we do have a code of ethics here. Maybe our rules are not akin to human laws, but we abide by them, and whoever breaks them, risks banishment. Sometimes even death. As for spies—our privacy is very important to us, and we don't take lightly to those who endanger it. But apart from that, we rarely kill humans. We just feed on them and make them forget. But we don't usually take their lives gratuitously."

"So kind of you," I said, wondering how he could find the whole thing so natural. "Why didn't Lillian make the spy forget, then?"

"First of all, I didn't say our ways were kind. Lions aren't kind to gazelles, either. They are just… lions." Clarence stared at me intently, with his head tilted, and I felt compelled to look away. "And second, I'm sure Lillian tried, but the spy's memories dated too far back for the oblivion to work. And, anyhow, spies are rarely shown mercy anywhere. It's the way things are, Mrs. Reighton."

"You all think so highly of yourselves, don't you?" I spat, channeling my frustration with Ludovic toward him. "You just take anything you want, because we humans are no more than worthless prey to you. You don't need to worry about war, hunger or poverty. Not even death. It must be great, being invulnerable. I envy you and your lack of problems, Sir."

Clarence tilted his head with surprise. "What

makes you think we're invulnerable? We can't even walk out in the sun. Does that sound *invulnerable* to you?"

He extended his hand and took Gabriel's pendant carefully. I jumped back, startled. So far, none of the vampires had dared to touch my amulet—I had begun to believe they were afraid of it.

"Can I tell you a story?" he said, caressing the tiny shapes at the end of each silver branch. "So you can ponder who should be afraid of who." I nodded with intrigue, and he continued. "When Ludovic was a young man, he was engaged to a girl from Naples. She was the daughter of a farmer who brought groceries to the baron's house where he and Francesca worked. Did he ever tell you about Bellissa?"

I shook my head, wondering why he was disclosing this out of the blue. I knew Ludovic and Clarence were close, but I hadn't had many opportunities to talk to the Englishman since my arrival.

"Bellissa was a witch. A *strega*, like they say in those parts. But Ludovic didn't know it." He paused. "And now, a question for you, Mrs. Reighton. Do you know who gave this to your husband?"

"No, but I have the feeling you are about to tell me."

"This is a *cimaruta*. A powerful witch's amulet.

Your husband didn't buy it in a store, and it didn't come to you by chance. Nothing happens by chance in the supernatural world, my dear."

I gulped, but I was determined to hold his maroon gaze. "What happened to Bellissa? Did they get married in the end?"

"They didn't."

"Why not?"

"Because she tried to kill his sister."

***

December 1946

When Elizabeth asked me to travel to New York for three days, it was like a godsend. She wanted me to meet some businessmen from Wall Street and close a deal in her name. Of course, she couldn't go herself, given her daytime limitations, so she chose me to do the hand-shaking and paper-signing.

I was exultant.

And slightly frightened.

The little village girl was going to New York to seal a deal with powerful capitalists.

If only my father could see me.

My train was leaving at nine in the evening. I informed Elizabeth I would walk to the station on my own, but she was inflexible about it.

"Listen, Julia," she had said, after a long discussion. "I've heard there's a crazy man walking around and pouncing on those he deems to be witches. I appreciate your desire for independence, but I need this deal to be sealed in a timely manner. You must allow Ludovic to escort you to the station and stop making my life impossible, will you please?"

"Can't Clarence go instead?" It felt puerile to ask, but the station was at least half an hour away. Too much time to spend with Ludovic, a man I found hopelessly repulsive and attractive at the same time. Clarence would have been a better, more neutral option.

"We value your opinion, Julia, but please try to remember who is in charge here," Elizabeth said with an impatient puff. "Clarence has his own business to attend to, while Ludovic is free tonight. He'll wait for you by the exit at eight thirty. Don't be late."

I wasn't late. In fact, I was fifteen minutes early. Sitting on my brand new leather suitcase by the gates of Saint Anne's cemetery, I waited for my chaperone to make his appearance. Temperatures had started to drop well below freezing at night, and I cursed myself for wearing only a calf-length coat and one thin pair of stockings. I should have overlapped at least two pairs to survive such cold.

When Ludovic's curls finally peeked out from behind the black angels' wings, I found him clad in a cozy-looking cloak and a top hat. He offered graciously to carry my suitcase, a proposal which I considered declining. I didn't feel comfortable accepting any help from someone who carried the surname Belak and had a talent for breaking people's necks in less than a millisecond. Still, he was very persuasive and, in the end, I gave up.

Sticking my red and frozen nose up in the air, I started to walk toward the station. Sometimes it was hard to sidestep the brownish heaps of plowed snow which glistened under the dim streetlights, but I did my best to carry myself gracefully.

"Julia," Ludovic said, stopping right in the middle of the sidewalk with his arms crossed in front of his wide chest. "Can you please look at me? I just asked you a question. Don't I even deserve a yes or no answer?"

Whatever question he was talking about, I must have missed it while actively hating him and his sister in my mind.

"Excuse me. I was thinking about the meeting tomorrow," I muttered, trying to bypass him and finding a huge heap of frozen snow blocking the path.

Ludovic didn't even balk: he just stood there like a pointless piece of urban furniture.

"If we don't hurry up, I'll miss the train, and Elizabeth will kill us both," I pointed out.

"I was asking you about the Sheens. Are you visiting that bookstore again? It's not necessary anymore, but if you insist, I could go with you. We could agree on a date now, and I'll mark it on my calendar."

Oh, he had a calendar? I wondered what for. A ridiculous picture appeared in my head, with Ludovic writing down his very important appointments: *"Monday: go hunt a couple of maidens; Tuesday: flirt with the witch so she stops asking about her dead husband; Wednesday: fly over the city and search for easy prey, maybe a couple of elderly ladies…"*

"Julia, are you listening to me?"

Impatiently, I crept on the heap of snow obstructing the sidewalk, fighting its slippery surface with my unpractical leather pumps until I managed to walk around Ludovic's massive figure without waiting for him to step aside. He raised a well-defined eyebrow, watching my climbing feat in utter disbelief.

"No, I'm not listening to you," I said sharply, "I can go on my own, and I will decide myself whether it's necessary or not. I don't need a nanny, thank you."

"There's a reason why I said that," he said, following me in long strides. "We found an interesting clue. Something you might like to hear. I've been trying to tell you for days, but you keep avoiding me."

"Surprise me." My voice was snarky, and I couldn't help it. "Or better yet, let me guess: they found Gabriel's remains in a remote Italian village on top of a rocky mountain."

Ludovic tipped his head to one side and blinked with visible surprise. "No?" he said, staring at me. "Where did that come from? Did you get hold of any new information I don't know about?"

Yes. A very interesting piece of news, for that matter, which involved him talking to his sister about diverting my attention from Gabriel's case. Of course, I didn't tell him.

"I don't know," I lied, "I just thought you were about to say something like that."

"No." He lowered his eyes. "I wrote to someone in Italy and asked her to do some research for us. Her name is Rosanna Bianchi. She just wrote back a few days ago, and I wanted to share with you what she told me."

Rosanna Bianchi. That was the name written on that envelope I found on the floor. In the end, I had slipped it under his door the next morning, without opening it. At least he wasn't making up the woman's name.

"Is she also a…?" I started to say. After all those months, it was funny that I still couldn't pronounce the word without wincing.

"A vampire?" He shook his head. "No. She's just a well-situated Roman lady who owes me a favor."

That sounded interesting, and it piqued my curiosity. I caved in. "And what did Mrs. Bianchi find out?"

I couldn't help it. I needed to know.

"She found a Gabriel Reighton's grave near Bitonto, in southwest Italy."

My legs became suddenly very heavy, and I had to lean on a streetlight to avoid toppling over.

"Well, that's a relief." I sighed, rubbing my cold and stiff arms.

"I'm glad it is," Ludovic said, though his tone was bitter, "but that's not all."

Chapter 7

Iulia

New York, December 1946

Another empty grave.

Mrs. Rosanna Bianchi had located Gabriel's grave in a cemetery near Bitonto. The name and date matched. She had even bribed a couple of undertakers—which made me seriously wonder about the nature and extent of the debt that this woman had contracted with Ludovic Belak— only to find that this grave, *too*, was empty.

As empty as the one in Saint Emery.

Sitting on the train and watching the lights of Emberbury fade in the distance, I couldn't help but wonder why.

Why would the army—or whoever had buried my husband—bother to provide a grave for him if they had no body to bury?

What had happened on that night of the 16th of August 1944, when my husband had been seen by his fellow soldiers for the last time?

And, of course: if Ludovic was trying to avert my attention away from the search, why on earth would he tell me such intriguing news? Because that wasn't helping his distraction cause much.

Upon our arrival at Emberbury Park Station, Ludovic had played the perfect gentleman and insisted on seeing me to my seat. I had allowed him to do it. We were already attracting our fair share of attention from the other travelers as it was: me, insisting on carrying the suitcase and practically tearing it from Ludovic's hands in the middle of the steps; and he, clad in his ridiculously old fashioned attire and looking at me like I was the most stubborn mule in the whole city.

He waved me off with his silken cylinder hat, and I sighed at the sight of that handsome, if thorny, man, who stood out among everyone else in the platform, and not only because of his clothes.

***

After getting off the train at New York Grand Central, I got lost at least three times trying to get out of the station. Finally, I hailed a cab and managed to reach my business meeting by a whisker.

Elizabeth and I had rehearsed each word I was supposed to say, and she had trained me on what to do and when. For someone who rarely went far from The Cloister, she was incredibly well-versed in business etiquette and trading customs, and her teaching allowed me to leave an impeccable impression on the other company's representatives.

The negotiations extended for a period of two-and-a-half days, and thanks to my vampire mentor's advice, I ended up closing the deal even more advantageously than expected. When I finally left that office on the twelfth floor of a gravestone-looking gray building, I was bursting with happiness and pride.

I could hardly believe that I'd been rubbing elbows with the big fish of Wall Street, all on my own and in a corporate environment devoid of female representatives—their secretary being the only exception. It was the most awe-inspiring achievement of my whole life, maybe discounting the successful *Green Luminescence* spell.

Feeling triumphant, I found an expensive-looking hotel and decided to treat myself to some coffee by a café window. I had more than five hours to get back to Grand Central, and I intended to relax while watching the crowded New York sidewalks and the streets full of modern vehicles. I would find a cozy place to sit and enjoy a warm beverage, sheltered from the cold and the snow.

As soon as I entered the café, a glass display cabinet full of sculptural cakes caught my eye. My mouth watered at the sight of dozens of cream and chocolate wonders gathered next to each other.

Even for a baker's daughter, the view was imposing.

From that moment on, I didn't care anymore for the skyscrapers or the well-dressed pedestrians outside. Not even for the sparkling diamonds on the store windows. I only had eyes for the hotel's magnificent selection of cakes, pastries and tartlets. After years of poverty and a long war under my belt, seeing all those luxurious baked goods in a row, and having the means to purchase whichever I wanted, was akin to having the Virgin Mary wave at me from Heaven.

I ordered a mouthwatering piece of cocoa *Sachertorte* with a sweet apricot filling. Even though I had heard of that Viennese delicacy, I had never had the opportunity to taste it myself, let alone make one, given the scarcity of sugar, eggs and butter during the war.

As I sank my fork into the upper chocolate layer, I thought with anguish about Ludovic and the evening he had brought me that splendid piece of white cake with the most delicate frosting I had ever savored. The Austrian *Sachertorte* was a rich umber tone, nearly black, which made it the total opposite of Ludovic's frosted marvel. I liked that. It was my personal way of declaring to all the ghosts fluttering around me that I, Julia Reighton, was going to be in charge of my own life from that moment on—and that included choosing whatever cake I wanted, whenever I wanted. If I craved the darkest chocolate cake available, that was my choice. If I could only love dead, dark and broken things, then so be it.

To dispel Ludovic's memory, which was spoiling my mood, I took a book out of my bag. It was a novel by Agatha Christie which I had found in the vampires' library. Spell books would rather wait for me on my nightstand in The Cloister, because one crazy witch hunter running after me was more than enough. I didn't want to attract more of those by reading witchcraft treaties in public places.

"I see you like mysteries."

An unknown woman sat down at my table without my permission, which in turn made me choke on the last chocolate crumbs.

After the cough subsided, I turned to find an elegant, curvy lady in her forties, enfolded in a myriad of sophisticated accessories.

"Have we met before?" I said, wiping my mouth with a perfectly ironed napkin. Seemingly, my fleeting moment of lone bliss was over.

"You are Mrs. Reighton," she said. "I saw you in a picture."

"A picture?" I hadn't posed for one in years. Unless she had got hold of my wedding portrait, she had to be mistaken. "I seriously doubt that. May I know your name?"

"Yes, of course. My name is Rosanna Bianchi," she extended a profusely bejeweled hand in my direction, and I took it reluctantly, suddenly aware of my unevenly trimmed nails. "You might have heard about me."

***

I had so many questions for the onyx-eyed woman in front of me that I didn't even know where to start.

"You don't mind me joining you, do you?" she was already waving at the waiter. Rosanna Bianchi didn't seem like the kind of person who would wait for permission to do anything.

"I thought you were in Italy." I scraped the whipped cream off my plate, gaping at Mrs. Bianchi with my mouth open.

"Ocean liners are quite fast nowadays." The waiter came back with a cocktail glass garnished with an olive, and she gulped down its contents before it even touched the table. "Another martini, please," she told him with a dazzling smile.

"What brings you here from so far away?" I asked.

"Business, as usual. I disembarked yesterday at New York harbor, and this is where I'm staying. I couldn't believe my eyes when I saw you sitting here! I've been looking forward to seeing your boss' offices for years, and it seems the Lord has finally awarded my patience by sending you directly to me. Are you going back to Emberbury soon?"

"Uh…" I hesitated. I found it worrying that

~ 82 ~

she was here to meet the vampires. Did they know about her arrival? I strongly doubted it. Should I tell her that I was about to leave for Grand Central? What if she followed me to The Cloister?

But then again, Elizabeth must be anxious to hear my news about the outcome of her business deal. Staying in New York until Rosanna Bianchi magically vanished didn't seem like a very good option, either.

"I am, actually," I said, choosing my words carefully as I took a sip of my coffee. "But my boss, as you call her, will be out of town for a couple of weeks. I doubt you will be able to meet her."

Rosanna Bianchi raised her thin and perfectly epilated eyebrows, squinting with curiosity. "Meet *her*? I thought you were working for Mr. Ludovic Belak."

She hadn't heard about Elizabeth? That was interesting. Obviously, her so-called *debts* must be related to some private affair concerning only Ludovic.

"Oh, yes, I meant Mr. Belak… and the rest of his associates. They are abroad too at the moment. I doubt your schedules will overlap." I was afraid of revealing too much. It was obvious from her words that she didn't have an appointment with anyone at The Cloister. Nobody there ever had any appointments with humans, as far as I knew.

"I have time to spare," she said, nestling comfortably in her bentwood chair. "I'll wait for their return."

"Have you ever met Mr. Belak in person?" I asked casually, trying to use the situation to my advantage and pry some useful information out of her.

"Yes, he came to Rome a couple of times," she said, tapping on the table lightly. She was surely fighting the urge to order yet another martini. "Such an interesting gentleman, isn't he?"

"Certainly," I said, trying to keep my voice aloof.

"His last letter was strange, though. I think it's time I find out who I'm borrowing favors from before I get myself into trouble. Exhuming bodies was never one of my favorite pastimes."

Exhuming bodies?

"I thought Gabriel's grave turned out to be empty," I said, feeling a sudden rush of emotion.

Mrs. Bianchi looked me up and down and hesitated.

"Mr. Belak asked me for a favor on your behalf, yes," she said, pinning back a stray wave of black hair. "And let me say, I found his request… *odd*, to put it mildly."

"I can imagine," I admitted. I was sitting on my hands, trying to hide my excitement. "Ludovic, I mean, Mr. Belak told me Gabriel's remains weren't in Italy, either."

"You are right," she said. "They weren't. Quite baffling indeed. Although not as much as the interest your… *boss* had in honoring such an odd request. Not to be harsh here, but your husband wasn't the only man who went missing during the war. There were thousands like him. Why would Mr. Belak call upon our past debts… to aid a mere *employee?*"

I shrugged. Ludovic had said that he wanted to help me find closure so I could leave my past behind and start a new life. Back then, I had believed him. Now I wasn't sure anymore.

"Because, if it wasn't so unlikely for someone as disciplined and genteel as Mr. Belak," she continued, holding her empty cocktail glass and staring at me from behind it, "I'd dare say his interest in you went beyond the professional."

Rosanna Bianchi paused to scan my face, but I didn't give her the pleasure of a surprised reaction. I remained motionless, smiling like the Mona Lisa and hoping for her to keep talking.

"He was very, very interested in finding out about Gabriel Reighton's fate. And let me tell you a little secret—" She batted her eyelashes and lowered her voice to a sensual purr. "—I got the feeling he'd rather find your husband… *dead.*"

***

That persistent Italian lady had seemingly set out to become my shadow. Feeling stalked, I tried to hide in the restroom for half an hour, hoping to give her the impression that I had left the restaurant through a back door. But after a while, she came knocking on the door of my stall, asking whether I was sick or I needed any help. She seemed quite capable of climbing up the door to check on my *wellbeing,* so I had to come out, eventually.

Rosanna Bianchi pestered me until I agreed to take a taxi together, then spent the whole ride flirting with the driver and pronouncing words wrong on purpose. She laughed sensually when the chauffeur pointed out that she was trying to pay in Italian liras, and I watched her performance in silence, hoping to learn something useful from her. Rosanna wasn't particularly pretty or young, but she had a magnetism about her that made everyone stare at her in awe.

As we boarded the train back to Emberbury, dread washed over me. Mrs. Bianchi had used her allure to get a seat in the same carriage as me, and now she was drilling me with her black eyes, which were round and watchful like an owl's, as she questioned me about my work at The Cloister. During the following hours, I learned that there existed a maximum number of times one could describe things as *nice* without sounding like a simpleton… or a liar.

Ludovic was supposed to pick me up at the station at 3 AM. The train stops succeeded each other relentlessly, just like Mrs. Bianchi's pointed questions. *What was Mr. Belak's company selling? Where had he gone on a business trip? Did he travel often? How old was he?*

Elizabeth had given me a few standard replies to satisfy our business partners in New York, but soon I ran out. Unless I found a way to get rid of Rosanna Bianchi, she was going to get very accurate answers much sooner than she thought.

An idea started to take shape in my head as the train slowed down to enter the city. Ludovic would be waiting for me at Emberbury Park Station. But I could get off the train one stop earlier, at Emberbury Central. That way, I would prevent my travel companion from meeting him against his will or, even worse, following us to The Cloister.

"Where do you live?" Rosanna asked, reapplying her lipstick like she expected the press to be waiting for her on the platform.

"I'll be staying in a hotel tonight." The lying was getting harder and harder. "My apartment is… undergoing renovations."

"Oh, that's great! We can stay in the same one, if you don't mind!"

Of course. Half an hour later, we checked into the nearest hotel. The fee was expensive, but Mrs. Bianchi didn't seem to mind. We were *so lucky* to get contiguous rooms.

When her bubbly chitchat finally relented, I wished her good night and sneaked into my accommodations with a sigh of relief. I didn't even sit on the bed, for fear of dozing off. Instead, I used the bathroom and waited on a chair, with my ear pressed to the thin wall, for signs of Rosanna falling asleep. When her light went off, I waited for twenty minutes and, finally, I grabbed my luggage and tiptoed out of the hotel, hoping she wouldn't hear me as I slipped out furtively.

Chapter 8

Julia

Emberbury, December 1946

The streets were dark and slippery, and I cursed Mrs. Rosanna Bianchi for stalking me and forcing me to walk the slushy sidewalks, exhausted and alone, in the hours before dawn.

The suitcase wasn't particularly heavy, but I was drowsy, and I tripped on a stick half-buried in the snow. I fell and swore aloud, relieved nobody could hear me.

To my surprise, a kind stranger offered me a hand and helped me stand up. When I looked at him, it felt like a bombshell dropping straight on my head.

"Mr. Sheen," I muttered in a shaky voice. It was a Mr. Sheen from the bookstore, but which one? The crazy one? Or the nice one?

"Isn't it a bit early for such a lovely lady to

roam the streets on her own?" His eyes narrowed maliciously. "Or should I say… *late?*"

I tried to calm my nerves. Just a couple of blocks more, and I would reach Saint Anne's cemetery. Then I would go to bed and forget about Rosanna Bianchi, the Sheens and all the nasty things that seemed to be going on lately.

"I had to work," I mumbled, picking up my handbag, which had flown directly into a half-frozen puddle. "And now, if you'll excuse me, I'd really like to go home."

When I tried to step away from him, he held my arm so tightly that I screamed.

"I said good night, Mr. Sheen," I snarled, removing his claws one by one with my hand.

The man smiled calmly and watched me handle his fingers. Meanwhile, his eyes did a psychotic wobble just like the one I had witnessed at the bookstore. By then, I knew for sure which of the Sheens I had the honor of facing.

The crazy one, of course.

"You must have a fascinating job, madam." He grabbed my wrists, and his long nails hurt me through the thin leather gloves. "Do you have time to accommodate yet another client? Or should I make a reservation in advance?"

I would have slapped him, but I couldn't get loose of his grip, so I did the best next thing: spit in his face.

"You won't talk to me like that, Mr. Sheen.

I'm going to call the police."

As he wiped his face, I quickly broke free from his grasp. Leaving the suitcase behind, I ran on the icy sidewalks, slipping and nearly falling several times. My handbag fell off my shoulder, but I didn't lose time retrieving it. My eyes were fixed on the fence of the park, which wasn't so far anymore.

There was a gap under the fence I knew about, and I slipped under it, hoping my pursuer wouldn't notice. Eluding the trees, I rushed desperately toward the graveyard gates, which glistened softly under the moonlight. When I reached them, I let my body crash against the iron doorway and fumbled with the handle in desperation.

The door was locked, and I had no key. It was in my handbag, lying somewhere in the middle of the street.

Mr. Sheen was approaching.

I would have to climb.

Heavy steps crushed the ice and fallen leaves of Saint Anne's park. I clambered up the ornate ironwork of the rusty iron doors and jumped in.

Breathless, I crouched behind a Celtic cross gravestone and remained completely still, waiting for him to walk on without seeing me.

Someone had lit a few candles around the angel mausoleum. In that abandoned graveyard, that could only mean one thing: a member of The Cloister was waiting for me nearby, which was very good news.

I would wait for Ed Sheen to go away and knock on the hatch which led to the catacombs. Hopefully, one of the vampires would open it from the inside, and I could go to sleep in peace.

When the cold blade touched my neck, I ingenuously mistook it for a snowflake.

Ed Sheen was holding a sharp knife, and he used it to pin me against the tombstone with all the weight of his body, as he pressed the blade against my throat.

"You don't seem so frightening now, witch." His breath smelled of onions and cheap alcohol.

"I'm not a witch," I grunted desperately, trying to push him aside. He was heavy, and the buckle of his belt was about to bore a hole in my hip.

Ed sneered. "Then how else could you know about Catalina Kodrinova, madam? No decent lady ever asked for any of those books."

"Put that knife away!" I screamed, trying in vain to sound calm. The last thing I wanted was to startle an armed maniac who was resting flat on my chest.

Ed Sheen lifted the blade from my neck and scooted over slightly. Then he slid the tip of the knife through my blouse and between my breasts, all the way down to my navel and below. Cold and terrified, I started to shiver.

"They say witches are lascivious creatures.

Would you agree, madam?" I shook my head, trying to burn him with my eyes. "But you smell of something else, too…" He sniffed the air and closed his eyes. "Undead creatures. Am I right? You reek of death so strongly that I'm surprised you're still breathing. Or aren't you? Because you really shouldn't be. This is a graveyard, after all."

While he spoke, I probed around, searching for a stick or a stone to hit him with. I found nothing.

"*Thou shalt not suffer a witch to live*," he said pensively, drawing circles with his blade right below the rim of my skirt. The blade cut my thighs, and I gasped.

"Not that old drivel again," someone growled in the background, and Ed Sheen's eyes widened with surprise when he realized we weren't alone anymore.

Ludovic.

As he pounced on Ed Sheen, the madman pressed the knife against my neck. Ludovic's eyes flashed with fury. When he opened his mouth, a sharp set of fangs glistened under the moon. He bit the man's throat ruthlessly, with the brutality of a beast. Ed Sheen screamed and pushed the knife deeper into my neck. The pain became so sharp that I thought I would faint. Blood gushed through the open wounds, mine and Ed's, and my lungs shrank under the man's weight, suffocating me.

"Let me go, or she dies," Ed Sheen gurgled.

I knew he wasn't lying, because his hand moved closer and everything grew darker.

Ludovic growled and detached his fangs from the man's neck with a wild head shake.

I heard Ed Sheen flee, and soon his steps became a soft rustle which blended with the night breeze.

When I drifted off, cradled in Ludovic's arms, the scent of bergamot filled the air, and I became one with the snow on the ground.

***

A mass of soft, silky locks brushed my cheek.

I woke up to a vampire licking the blood on my neck, and terror paralyzed me.

Holding my breath, I pretended to be asleep, remembering the viciousness in Ludovic's eyes when he had bit Ed Sheen. I pressed my eyes together, commanding the fog to vacate my brain.

A soft, warm fabric covered the gravestone. Velvet. Black velvet for sure. I caressed it discreetly, waiting languidly for the *coup de grâce*. I was still lying over a stone in Saint Anne's graveyard, surrounded by candles, and a deadly vampire was leaning over me, propped on his arms and knees.

Ludovic's lips trailed from my ear to my shoulder, and I lay still on the ground, expectant. His breaths were deep, but far apart, and his nose traveled up my throat until his eyes aligned with mine.

Now he knew I was conscious.

"I searched for you like a madman," he whispered in my ear, and I moaned when his hair tickled my skin once again.

My shirt was torn and sticky, and I reached over to touch the cuts on my throat.

They were gone.

The pain, the blood, everything was gone.

His kisses had sealed my wounds.

Was he there to kill me or to heal me?

Lethal as he was, I hadn't felt more attracted to a man in my whole life.

Ludovic moved aside and sat on the ground next to me, watchful. "He won't live to see another dawn," he said quietly.

I had to make a herculean effort to comprehend he was talking about Ed Sheen.

"And what about me?" I asked, my voice trembling.

"What do you mean, my dear?" he said, leaning down to brush the hair away from my face and sending quivers through my whole body.

"Will I live to see another sunrise?" I said quietly.

Ludovic lowered his voice, answering with his eyes half-closed. "You, my dear Julia, will see the sun rise in the sky for as long as I'm here to watch over you." He dropped a soft kiss on my forehead. "And when there are no more sunrises left, I will offer you all the sunsets. If you want them."

***

When we disentangled ourselves from each other, the black sky had started to turn into a dim shade of purple. I kissed Ludovic once again and inhaled his citrus fragrance. Soon, the burning rays of the sun would force us to leave our nook behind the Celtic cross tombstone. We would hide in the catacombs, and I would carry on doing mundane tasks. Maybe even pretend nothing happened, just like the first time we kissed.

But until that moment came, I would run my fingers over those silken locks, darker than the Black Sea, and try to engrave that last hour in my mind. That way, I would be able to bring it out later, whenever life turned gloomy and I needed fond memories to keep myself afloat.

"I need to go inside," he murmured softly, but he didn't move an inch. We were lying side to side on the ground, curled up among the folds of his cloak. Surprisingly, I wasn't cold anymore. When I thought he was about to drink my blood, he had been licking my wounds and sealing them. Now they were gone, and all I felt was bliss.

It was odd to feel happy, in the most unexpected of all places, with the most unexpected companion.

Sitting up, I buttoned up my coat over the

torn shirt and stared at the flames of the candles around us.

"Did you light them?" I asked him, taking one of them in my hands. I sheltered the flickering flame with the palm of my hand. It was a frail little thing. Just like me. A tiny, wavering object, but—let it fall on dry leaf litter, and it could start a colossal fire.

He nodded. "I did, yes. In case you got lost," he said with an oddly shy shrug.

"How could I get lost on my way home?"

Ludovic smiled and hugged me. "Home," he repeated warmly.

A small animal, maybe a rabbit, leaped across the opposite side of the cemetery, scattering leaves and frost around it. A few more followed, and Ludovic flinched.

"Don't worry. It's just a couple of bunnies," I said, pulling him back into my arms.

"They must be really large bunnies," he said, puzzled.

When I turned around, the wooden stake was already hovering over his head.

Ed Sheen was back and ready to kill.

With the noise of the leaping animals, we hadn't heard him coming.

Swiftly, I took the stake by its lower end and pulled at it with all my strength. Meanwhile, Ludovic stood up and tried to dodge the attack. But Ed was faster, and the stake sank into the vampire's side, missing his heart. Ludovic tripped and fell to the floor, curled up in a ball.

Gasping, I hesitated for a second between rushing to help him and finding a sharp weapon.

Ed sauntered smugly toward Ludovic, who was struggling to stand up. The bookseller lifted the stake in the air once again and grinned.

"Didn't expect the vampire hunter back so soon?" he said with delight. "Couldn't miss out on the opportunity of killing a bloodsucker and a witch in one single go."

Desperate, I grabbed one of the candles, inhaled deeply and aimed it at Ed Sheen.

"*Viridi Lux*!" I shouted and threw it in his direction.

The candle hit the stake he was holding and set it alight. A green glow surrounded the wooden stick, and Ed released it in an involuntary reflex.

It was just the diversion that Ludovic needed. As he stood up, I charged from the other side. Throwing myself like a cannonball on the hunter, I managed to knock Ed to the floor, while Ludovic jumped on his neck.

This time, there was no mercy left for Mr. Sheen. Before I could look aside, Ludovic had sunk his fangs into the bookseller's throat, and I watched as though hypnotized as the man lost all color in his cheeks and finally hit the ground like a dead weight.

At that very moment, the first ray of sun peeked from among the clouds, and Ludovic vanished into a cloud of smoke, shifting into a magnificent black raven which flew into the treetops.

I remained alone with Ed Sheen's inert body, standing among the old graves on a cold blanket of snow. When I thought the morning couldn't have a worse start, a gasp informed me that I wasn't as lonely in the cemetery as I had imagined.

Rosanna Bianchi was slumping on the other side of the gate, holding both hands over her mouth and a grimace of horror distorted her dignified face.

Chapter 9

Julia

Emberbury, December 1946

Rosanna Bianchi ran away, and I went back to the catacombs, followed by Ludovic.

Soon, he materialized next to me. A terrified look appeared on his face when he saw Elizabeth standing in the hall, with her arms crossed and a deep frown marring her forehead.

"Who is that woman, and why did you let her run away?" She said furiously. "How could you allow her to flee? She saw you kill a man. Not only that, she knows the location of our dwelling!"

"Elizabeth, I can explain," Ludovic said. His voice was shaking, which was rare for him. "Her name is Rosanna Bianchi. I met her in Italy seven years ago. She…" He paused and took a deep breath. "She found out I was a vampire. But she never told anyone. I know for certain she can be trusted."

I could hardly believe what I was hearing, and Elizabeth even less, judging by her expression.

"I'm appalled at your reckless behavior," she said after a while, shaking her head in disbelief.

After that, her sentence was quick and unwavering.

The only sacred thing in The Cloister was Elizabeth's set of rules. It was forbidden for all outsiders to learn about the clan and its whereabouts.

Rosanna knew too much and, after seven years, it was too late to make her forget.

She would have to die.

After pronouncing her verdict, Elizabeth left and Ludovic entered Francesca's room, still covered in blood after the fight with Ed Sheen. I waited in a corner of the hall, listening to their conversation.

That was when the screaming started.

Francesca's cries were ear piercing, and there was something visceral about the way she bellowed; something completely irrational, which made my skin tingle and the thinnest of hairs stand on end.

"Elizabeth wants her dead," Ludovic said in a shaky voice, as he twisted his hands with dismay. "She has known about me for too long. I shouldn't have allowed it, but... you know why I did it. And now we can't make her forget seven years of her life."

Francesca screeched, pulling at her hair. She plucked out a whole tuft of golden curls and tossed it to the floor. It spread over the tiles like a cloud of jinxed fairy dust.

"I'm so sorry, sister. I'm sorry," Ludovic said, and something like a tear escaped his eyes.

I tried to make myself inconspicuous as I stared at both vampires, brother and sister. Francesca's face was almost unrecognizable due to sorrow, and Ludovic held her with love and devotion so deep that it filled the whole room. But his grip was also firm. Firm enough to keep the petite woman from destroying everything that surrounded her… and herself.

For me, it was hard to understand the reaction of the Belaks to Rosanna's condemnation. As I had come to learn, killing humans wasn't something they didn't do in The Cloister. They just didn't do it *often*.

Francesca hugged her brother, then lifted him like a feather and sent him flying across the hall. As he tried to stand up, she ran after him, with her eyes glowing like red embers. She smashed a chair and tore one of its legs. Then she tried to stake her brother's chest with it.

Elizabeth reappeared just in time to stop her.

Once the screaming calmed down, the vampire girl's eyes caught sight of me cowering on the other side of the corridor.

She opened her mouth and hissed, threatening me with her protruding fangs.

"You!" she shouted, pointing at me with a

long, bony finger. "It was all because of you!"

She tried to attack me, but three other vampires ran to stop her, alerted by the belligerent sounds. It took their joint efforts to hold back the crazed Francesca, who bit them and kicked everything and everyone, behaving like the devil itself.

It wasn't until Elizabeth lifted the stake over Francesca's head that the tiny blonde girl collapsed in a heap on the floor and started to sob.

"You know the rules," Elizabeth said firmly. There was a slight tinge of sadness in her voice. "No exceptions. I'm sorry, Francesca. Your brother shouldn't have revealed so much. If she can't forget, Mrs. Bianchi must die. Otherwise, it will be both of you."

***

Elizabeth ordered Ludovic to take care of Rosanna Bianchi. She blamed him for luring her into the catacombs by contacting her thoughtlessly for many years, sharing too much personal information. I was supposed to be an accomplice, too. My mission would be to lure Mrs. Bianchi to a dark place on the next evening, so that Ludovic could quickly settle the matter for good.

Secretly, I feared Francesca was right, and everything was my fault. My wish to find out about Gabriel's death had caused a dreadful mess. I had finally realized that Gabriel was dead, wherever he was, and no amount of searching would bring him back to life: the whole quest had been pointless. On the other hand, Rosanna Bianchi was just an innocent *living* woman who had tried to help me. I had led her to a vampire nest, and unfortunately, she had seen too much.

Francesca kept sulking, and I overheard Lillian's snickering suggestion to chain her in a dungeon until she calmed down.

I spent the next day feeling heavy-hearted, as one single question rattled around in my mind: why had Francesca lost her mind about Mrs. Bianchi, a foreign woman she had never met?

***

"Let's go," Ludovic said somberly as soon as night fell over Emberbury. We walked up the stairs together in silence, our steps resonating as we got closer to the surface.

A knot had nestled in my throat, hindering my ability to speak. The way he glanced at me, he wasn't feeling much cheerier, either.

"Take her to dinner first," he said, "make it a nice evening for her. Answer all her questions. It doesn't matter anymore."

Ludovic walked with his shoulders slumped, so much so that they barely held his rich velvet cloak in place. Even though he wasn't as affected as

Francesca, his blue gaze was fuzzy and distracted.

"I wish I hadn't started this," I said, shaking my head. "It's all my fault."

"No, it isn't," he said with a deep sigh. "It had nothing to do with you. She would have come, sooner or later. I engaged too much with her. I shouldn't have, but I felt obliged to."

"Why? What did you do?"

"She was in trouble at the beginning of the war, and I offered her my help. I should have done it anonymously, but I was too eager to meet her."

At that moment, I could only think of one reason why a man would do such a thing, and it made me feel oddly jealous of Mrs. Bianchi.

"You loved her," I stated, remembering how everyone had stared at Rosanna's graceful gait on the crowded streets of New York.

Ludovic smiled weakly and shook his head. "Yes, but not the way you think."

I tilted my head in a silent question, and he brushed a lock of hair from my face.

"I love her because she's part of our family. She's Francesca's great-granddaughter. But Rosanna doesn't know it."

Chapter 10

Emberbury, December 1946

I felt like a hangman leading her victim to the gallows.

Rosanna Bianchi was already waiting for me in the restaurant, dressed impeccably in an indigo dress with a flared skirt, her hair adorned with a tasteful peacock feather headpiece.

"I thought he was coming too," she said, looking disappointed. I had called the hotel and left a message with the concierge, inviting her to dinner at one of the finest restaurants in the city.

"He… couldn't make it, but you will see him later," I said, an edge of dread in my voice. My stomach churned.

"I know what he is," she said, looking intently into my eyes. "I have known since he appeared at my doorstep in the fall of 1939. I wasn't afraid then, and I'm not now." I admired her bravery. If only she knew what awaited her. "Are you?"

I shook my head. "I have no reason to be."

"I thought so," she said, laying the stiff white napkin carefully over her lap. "Would you like to know how I guessed? Because it wasn't for lack of discretion on his part, rest assured."

"Tell me," I said quietly.

"Your husband's isn't the only empty grave in the south of Italy. My great-grandmother, Angela, was found in a basket at a rich family's door. It was a badly kept secret in town, because her adoptive mother hadn't been able to have any children for years, and she was never seen pregnant. My mother was always curious to find out where Angela came from. Everybody said she must have been an unwanted baby, a bastard."

It wasn't hard to imagine who could have been Angela's mother, and I felt the tears gathering under my eyelids.

"Please," Rosanna said, waving as to dispel the heavy spirits. "Those things happened often then. Nothing extraordinary. My great-grandmother, Angela, was lucky to find a good family who raised her. But my mother was nosy. She spent most of her time at church, but she rarely went there to pray. What she did was gossip, read death records and stroll around cemeteries instead. She kept searching for Angela's mother. And one day she ran across Francesca and Ludovic Belak's story. Some elderly ladies from a village near Naples still remembered it. And it went like this…”

The waiter served our entrées, and Rosanna thanked him with a smile before continuing.

“Francesca was the daughter of a Napolitana and a Slavic man. A true beauty, too much for her own good. She worked as a governess, teaching a widowed baronet’s daughter, and the widower became infatuated with her. Angela was probably the widower’s daughter, conceived forcefully and in sin. After baby Angela was born, the poor young mother was forced to get rid of her.”

“That’s so terribly sad.” I slumped in my seat, starting to understand Francesca’s deep sorrow.

“It is indeed. But the story didn’t end there. Francesca left the job in the house and—their words, not mine—she chose the way to perdition. She was seen doing many indecorous things after that, and her brother severed all ties with her, kept his honest job as a cook and got engaged to a decent farmer’s daughter. But eventually, the depraved widower was found murdered. An atrocious death, they say. They found him in his bed, completely dismembered and drained of all his blood. Bad tongues say that Francesca got a devil inside her, in punishment for her sins. Not only that, but she also dragged her brother to hell with her. Soon after the widower’s death, both Belaks fled the village and were never seen again. But their tomb is there today, somewhere in the vicinity of Naples, and…” She smiled. “Guess what.”

"It's empty."

The waiter took away the entrées and served the second course. I lifted my fork, then put it back immediately. I wasn't hungry at all.

"The Belak tomb is also empty, yes." Rosanna still had a healthy appetite, though, and ate with glee, oblivious to the fate awaiting her outside the restaurant. "But this isn't the most interesting part of my story, at least not for you."

She made a dramatic pause to look into my eyes, and for the first time, I noticed her uncanny resemblance to Ludovic. She had the same hair, the same eyebrows. Even the same nose. Strange, how human traits were passed down and inherited in the most unexpected ways. "Before the war started, I was a widow just like you. I had nothing left. That was when I got a letter from an unknown man called Ludovic Belak who lived abroad."

"He offered to help you."

"He sent money, yes. But then he also came to see where I lived and sent workers to rebuild my derelict house and advisors to teach me to run my deceased husband's business on my own. He never asked for anything back. You can imagine, I was first expecting something sinister. But I took the money anyway, because I didn't see the point in dying of hunger."

"I think I know the rest of the story," I said, pushing the plate away. The smell of food made me dizzy.

"You do. When my mother died, five years ago, I read all her notes and connected the dots. I asked Ludovic, but he denied it. But, in my heart, I always knew the truth."

"I see."

"And then, there's the part I didn't tell you in New York," she said mischievously. "The part concerning your husband. Though I'm not sure you'll be happy to hear what I'm about to say."

"Whatever it is, I'm sure I'd love to know," I said, my words sounding much truer than they actually were.

"As you wish," she said, "but don't say I didn't warn you."

She licked her spoon with delight, then lowered her voice to a conspiratorial tone. "Gabriel Reighton is still alive."

Chapter 11

Julia

Emberbury, December 1946

Gabriel was alive.

My *husband* was alive.

I should be jubilant, possibly dancing with joy, because I wasn't a war widow anymore.

And suddenly all I could think was Ludovic Belak.

Ludovic Belak… and the job I was about to lose.

No more closing business deals for Elizabeth.

No more rubbing shoulders with the corporate big fish.

And no more spells or fancy cakes at midnight.

I'd just go back to being Gabriel's wife in Saint Emery and bear his children, live in a moldy rental house with a red tile roof, and return to my old workdays behind the assembly line. In the evenings, I would sew for a couple of hours and chat with the neighbors, and dream about a past when I made things glow, just like Mrs. Marie Curie.

I would pretend I was still normal.

Pretend I was still *just Julia*.

The sudden realization that it was no longer the life I wanted was so painful that it squeezed all the air out of my chest, impeding me from speaking.

"That's…" I tried to speak, but only tears came out. "That's wonderful," I said with a sniff.

"Before you lift up your spirits too much," Rosanna continued, possibly misunderstanding my dismay for excitement, "you may want to hear the rest."

By then, I was already trembling in my chair. When Rosanna offered me her glass of vodka, I washed it down in one single go but felt no relief afterwards.

"Gabriel changed his name to Gabriele Puglisi," Rosanna was saying, "he feigned his death and ran away to Sicily with his Italian mistress." She carefully watched my reaction, but at that point, I didn't really care whether he had run away with a mistress or a goat, so long as he wasn't coming back for me. "He's living now on the island with her, and I think they even have a child. She's the village's witch, by the way. A real *strega!* Can you imagine?"

My body stopped trembling abruptly.

I waved for the waiter to bring me some water and waited for him with my eyes closed.

"I'm so sorry," Rosanna said, "I know it must be a lot to take in. That's why I initially decided not to tell you. Maybe it would have been easier to accept that he was just dead."

When I stood up and hugged Rosanna Bianchi, she was so perplexed that she froze as though she had turned into a stone statue.

"You can't imagine how happy your words have made me," I said, and I kissed Rosanna Bianchi, possibly for the last time ever.

Chapter 12

Julia

Emberbury, December 1946

"Ludovic is going to kill you," I told Rosanna. We were the last guests left in the restaurant, and the waiter was peeking at us warily from the kitchen window. If we didn't get out soon, he might boot us on his own. "But I know for certain that he doesn't want to."

This was Rosanna Bianchi's turn to be shocked. Her confident mask fell apart for a second, giving me a glimpse of the sensitive woman behind it.

"He wouldn't do that."

"He has no choice."

Even pronouncing the words was painful.

"Whatever my fate, I'm willing to face it," she said, standing up from the chair. The waiter rushed to help us with our coats, a relieved smile softening his features.

"Where?" Rosanna asked, like we were just going for a pleasant walk.

"The park. There's a dark, hidden spot behind the fountain. We should meet him there."

"You will think I'm crazy, but I can't wait to see him again. My great-grandmother's brother. I so wish I could see her, too."

When we reached the gates, I showed Rosanna the broken stretch of fence, and we both sneaked underneath it.

"Let me go first," I said, "I'll talk to him."

Rosanna nodded and cleaned the snow off a bench, then sat down to wait.

Ludovic was standing behind the fountain, holding one hand in the other with his eyes closed.

"We're here," I whispered, and he opened his eyes with a heavy exhalation.

"I can't do this to Francesca," he said, and I noticed his eyes were misty.

"Then let Rosanna go. I'll tell Elizabeth that you killed her. She will never find out."

His laughter was bitter. "Of course she'll find out. She'll kill me, and then you. There are very few rules in the Cloister, but we are supposed to follow them all or leave. Liars and traitors are not welcome here. And you know what? I don't even resent her. You have no idea how things were before, and what lengths Elizabeth had to go to protect us all. Ed Sheen was an amateur in comparison to the hunters of the past."

I nodded, hoping one day I'd get to hear those stories too.

"Maybe Rosanna could run away with Francesca," I said in a thin voice.

"No. Everything that happened was my fault. I can't let Francesca pay for my mistakes. I became what I am to protect my sister," he said quietly. "Did you know that a witch tried to kill her because she was a vampire? A witch I trusted. You can imagine why it was so hard for me to welcome another witch into our lives."

"Clarence told me," I said.

"Did he? Did he also tell you that, on that very day, I asked Francesca to turn me? She didn't want to, but I made her do it." He sighed. "And even though I promised to guard her, I've brought the worst possible fate upon her and her offspring. She will never forgive me, and I will never forgive myself. My whole life and the promises I made… everything will turn to nothing. But what am I to do? We also made a promise to Elizabeth, and everyone in The Cloister owes their life to her, in one way or another. So what can I do, Julia? What should I do?" his voice broke into a soft sob, and my hands found his. The comforting scent of tangerine and bergamot swathed me, and I knew immediately what we had to do. It just hurt too much to say it.

But I had to.

"You are going to run away. Go away with Rosanna. Disappear. Go back to Italy. Change your name. Elizabeth won't go after you. If she's going to banish you, you can just do it yourself. That should do just as fine."

"I considered that possibility," he said, swallowing hard. "And one year ago, I would have chosen that option without further ado. Today, though…"

Ludovic paused abruptly and extended his arms to bring me closer to his chest.

"If you kill Rosanna, you will shoulder that burden for all eternity. And so will I."

He hugged me so tight that I could hardly breathe, and I returned the hug with my eyes closed. I wrapped my hands around his neck, making him lower his face to my height. Once he was just an inch away from me, I kissed him passionately, putting into that kiss all the tears and the passion and the love I had missed and lost in my life. And he returned the kiss with such ferocity, such hunger, that I wondered for a second whether he was just about to bite my neck and drain the life out of my veins.

Not that I would have minded.

The sound of Rosanna clearing her throat on the other side of the fountain broke the spell of the moment. I released Ludovic and wiped my eyes on my sleeve.

"I'm sorry," Rosanna said, stepping

prudently in our direction. "I didn't mean to interrupt. It's just… if this has to end… you know, my nerves are strong, but I'm not made of steel."

Ludovic bowed in her direction.

"Mrs. Bianchi," he said knowingly.

Rosanna nodded, her lower lip twitching almost imperceptibly. "Uncle," she whispered. "Whatever you have to do, do it fast. I don't have the entire night."

Chapter 13

Iulia

Ludovic and Rosanna left.

Only the footprints on the snow remained, as feeble proof that the whole evening hadn't been the product of my feverish imagination.

The red ruby ring on my thumb was cold against my skin, and it reminded me of Ludovic's strong, chilly hands. When I touched it, I could almost relive our last kiss and the moment he had put it on my finger. A family heirloom of the Belaks, he had presented me with the shiny crimson stone together with the promise to come back and retrieve it one day.

"Just a loan," he had said, trying to make light of the situation.

Rosanna Bianchi's life would be spared, but mine had just been severed for the second time after Gabriel's pretended death.

It was almost humorous that Mrs. Bianchi, as

soon as she had fathomed what was taking place before her eyes, had been the one trying to convince Ludovic to finish the job Elizabeth had entrusted him with.

"Just do whatever you have to do and put all of us out of this misery," Rosanna had said bravely, with her arms crossed over her abundant bosom.

I had stood there, divided between my deep affection for Ludovic and the compassion I felt for that innocent woman.

"I'll go back with Rosanna, make sure her identity is fully erased," Ludovic had said, his voice husky. "Then I'll stay in Italy for a couple of decades, wait for things to calm down. We'll try to lie low, be discreet. It won't be easy, but we'll survive. Once we get through the first years, things will become easier. Elizabeth will gradually stop searching for us."

A couple of decades, he had said. It should be enough to soften Elizabeth's heart.

And to break mine.

"Make sure you talk to Francesca in private and explain everything to her. She has suffered enough."

Overwhelmed, I had just nodded. I knew we were doing the right thing. But why did it have to be so hard?

"It's too dangerous for you to come with us now, and you have much to do here anyway," he had said.

That much was true. Spending half of my mortal life in hiding would deprive me of the time and means to study magic. And deep in my heart, I knew that was the thing I wanted the most.

"I'll meet you on the other side, my darling," Ludovic had whispered into my ear before leaving.

"There's not such a place. I don't believe in anything anymore."

"Oh, but there is. I know… because I have been there. I'll come back for you, if you don't forget about me in the meantime."

I was trying not to cry, but he was making it really tough.

"Maybe a decade means nothing to you," I said, surrendering to the tears. "But what about me?"

"You have a purpose here, Julia," he said, kissing the top of my head. "There's so much waiting for you. I saw that gleam in your eyes when you cast your first spell. That was a glow of true joy and pride, and I can't take that away from you in exchange for the life of an outlaw. You weren't born just to be someone's wife or someone's shadow. You are a descendant of the witches of old, and there's so much magic slumbering inside of you, waiting to be set ablaze, that I can't tie you to my fate and forego that."

I wanted to tell him that he was foolish, and no, there was nothing I wanted more than to follow him to wherever he was going, but I knew that wasn't the truth.

The enigmatic future The Cloister had just opened up for me was too enticing, too tempting, and it hurt just to think about abandoning everything so soon. Definitely, I wouldn't have given any of that away for Gabriel, the husband who had deserted me and his country and never bothered to write back.

But I would have for Ludovic.

Still, he was right.

I wasn't ready yet.

"But all those lost years, Ludovic. I can't stand the thought."

"We will make up for lost time. I will come back for you: in a few years, when things settle down. In the meanwhile, you will have enough time to study your magic books. Trust me. All will be well."

Ludovic kissed me once more, his eyes glittering with sparkles of turquoise light. Rosanna was waiting for him by the gate, her back toward us in a futile attempt to give us an illusion of privacy.

"I just broke all the rules for my sister," he said, holding my gaze, "I wouldn't mind doing it for the woman I love, too."

Was he trying to imply…?

"Are you offering me what I think you are?"

"When you're ready, if you ever are," he said, hugging me for one last time, "just call me, and I will find you. Wherever you are."

Epilogue

My name is Julia, and I am not a war widow, nor a witch, nor a vampire bride.

But one day I will be all three of them, and I will regret none.

Up until then, I vow to live my life fully, make things disappear, glow and explode, and accept my fate and whatever it brings, for the present is a gift, and the future is not granted to any of us, mortal or immortal.

May the magic stay with you always.

The story continues in the next book in the series, Stray Witch. Turn the page to read the first chapters for free!

You'll also find a QR code to download a special thank-you gift for reading this story.

Julia has vanished from The Cloister, leaving behind secrets that refuse to stay buried...

Meanwhile, Alba—the so-called 'stray witch'—is trying to escape the ruins of her life. A failing marriage, a string of bad decisions, and a world closing in on her. The good news? She's a witch. The bad? She doesn't even know it.

Enter Clarence, a charming but tormented vampire, whose arrival throws Alba's already chaotic existence into disarray. As the vampires of Emberbury draw her into their dark and dangerous world, Alba discovers that sometimes the scariest monster isn't the one with fangs—it's the one staring back at you in the mirror.

Discover how Alba's journey intertwines with Julia's fate in Stray Witch, the next chapter in the Vampires of Emberbury saga.

Stray Witch

Prologue

One of the rare perks of being a creature of darkness was the remarkable ability to behold the city from above, with its buildings glistening under the blazing sun like jewels strung in a necklace. If I spread my wings, I could soar above the silver streets and study the habits of the busy, distracted humans, who went about their days in oblivious bliss.

A long time ago, I had been one of them.

Unfortunately, I didn't hold many fond memories of those days, and flying kept my mind busy enough to forget, at least for the brief duration of each journey, the misfortunes and depravities of my past. So much blood had been shed to feed the monsters—the monsters like us.

Volunteering for the search had allowed me many years of perfect distraction, for it wasn't a light task: some in The Cloister said there were no strays left and whined that the quest would be in vain. But I had been gifted with the patience of the immortal, and I pursued my goal until one day, the wind brought me the bitter scent of witches' blood. Feelings of ambivalence flooded my chest when I realized my work would soon be done.

There she was, so lovely in her humble simplicity. So ordinary, so frail. *Not for long,* I told myself.

I turned back to The Cloister to relay my news to the others. They would be relieved. But I? Not so much. I enjoyed the thrill of a good quest. And I hated idleness.

When I knocked on the queen's door, she was already expecting me.

"I found her," I said with a slight bow.

Elizabeth nodded and started to get ready for the new guest.

"We need to act fast," she said. "Before anyone else finds her, too."

Chapter 1

Alba

"I want a divorce," Mark said, smoothing the silk tie which peeped out of his perfectly tailored blazer. "Actually, I just filed the paperwork this morning."

Despite the warm summer morning, I felt something turn to ice inside my chest. Divorce had been on his lips many times before, but I hadn't expected him to just go and file the paperwork without telling me first.

Not that he hadn't mentioned it before—he used divorce threats as the ultimate approach to get his way. But Mark was an attorney, after all, so I had always thought that marriage termination must be a natural and intrinsic part of his life; a singular kind of small-talk reserved for those who paced the halls of courthouses with coffee in paper cups and watches which cost more than an average person's car.

Still, it took me by surprise because the pressure had dropped for a while, as I had tried really hard to please him, foregoing my own wishes and naively believing we could reach a truce and be happy *again*.

Although *again* was a bit of a stretch. I couldn't really recall one single happy day in this doomed union of ours. And somehow, I sensed it was my fault for not being the beautiful, patient, sexy creature he had expected. I had fooled him with my ephemeral youth and carelessness, and he was good at reminding me about it every single day.

Mark left the room, closing the door carefully. *Things* should be treated with respect, he used to say.

A cool draft swept across the room as the door clicked into place. It carried the smell of freshly cut wood and rusty iron. A raven had been sitting on a branch of the magnolia tree in our garden while Mark spoke. I closed the window, feeling cold and somehow spied upon by the silent dark bird. I had seen it before, and it had bizarre eyes. Too profound and bright for a simple bird, so much so that it made me think of grandma's stories about ghosts and demons inhabiting foreign bodies.

I startled as I tripped on a naked, legless Barbie, then bent down to pick it up, mulling absentmindedly about how much Mark hated finding toys lying on the floor. He always got edgy and raised his voice, or worse. A good way to keep our frail, homely harmony was to find bothersome items before he did.

So that was it. Mark had finally thrown the dreaded D-bomb at me, not caring that I stood in front of an ironing board holding one of his luxurious French couture shirts, the one he would wear tonight in order to impress his boss. My hand lingered on the iron for a couple of seconds too long, and the satisfying smell of burned fabric filled the room, as a brownish triangular mark formed on the back of the garment. It had cute, symmetrical rows of dots on each side: almost too nice. I wished I could just breathe fire like a dragon and burn his whole business wardrobe at once, forcing him to present himself in front of his colleagues wearing a greasy paper bag. My fingertips started to tingle with excitement at the thought, as they usually did when I held back my anger. In my late twenties, I was almost too young to grow gray hairs, but still, I had a few: a mute testimony of the hundreds of arguments it had taken to remain sane in my *better* half's company.

I could envision his fury when he found out about the shirt later that evening, and my pulse accelerated, fearing his reaction.

Breathe, Alba, breathe.

He's just a man. An ordinary human, just like you. The law doesn't allow him to harm you. And you know that Law *is his only true love.*

I counted up to eight with each exhale.

There were other forms of torture which didn't leave marks, and my darling husband excelled at all of them.

"I'll find a way," I told myself.

I sat on the bed, reaching for my phone, just to throw it back among the pillows as I realized I had nobody to call. I was about to divorce an attorney at law, and one who wanted to destroy my life at that. My worst nightmares looked like fairy tales in comparison.

Not that my nightmares hadn't warned me about Mark, time and again. But I had always been good at ignoring my dreams, although it didn't do much good in the long run.

Just as I was digging through a drawer in search of a tissue to blow my nose—not that I was crying, but the magnolias were in full bloom and spreading nasty pollen all over Emberbury—my five-year-old daughter, Katie, came into the room. Her arms were full of the remainders of a torn book, and she was followed by a black stray cat that she and her sister had found a couple of weeks ago, roaming in the garden.

The animal had gold and purple eyes, an uncommon trait in black cats. I figured it must be a very rare and expensive cat breed—like that hairless beast my neighbor, May, had bought her son for the price of a spa weekend in Bali—and someone must be searching frantically for it in our fine neighborhood.

"Mommy, Iris tore the cover of my favorite book. Can you glue it back?"

"Let me see, maybe I can," I said, caressing my girl's head as I inconspicuously wiped my nose right after hers, with the same tissue.

The book was a glitter hardback monstrosity, full of pink and purple illustrations of witches and fairies. I found some glue in a drawer, put the pieces together and pressed them firmly. "Now we wait for it to get dry, okay?"

I eyed the black cat, which had jumped on Mark's shirts and was purring and kneading them. Hopefully, it would leave plenty of claw marks all over the costly Egyptian cotton.

"Did you name it already?" I asked, telling myself we had to adopt that animal, if only to upset Mark.

"Yes, mommy! She's Miss Jilly now. Like the

witch from my book."

"Great name."

"Thank you, mommy," Katie said, kissing my cheek, "You know," she said, giving me a mysterious look. "I think you are just like Miss Jilly. The witch, not the kitty," She pointed at the cat, who was now trying to remove a button from one of the shirts with its bare teeth. I considered the possibility of stopping her, but I was enjoying the sight too much.

"Oh, really?" I smiled at the occurrence. I had yet to grow warts on my nose and get myself a flying broom, but hey, why not? At least I didn't remind her of a gryphon.

"Yes, you always make everything good again. I love you, mommy."

Then she hugged me with her tiny arms and left with the book.

I made a prodigious effort not to start weeping like a willow before my daughter and her elusive cat until they were out of sight.

"*Almost* everything," I said quietly to myself, as I daydreamed about being Miss Jilly and fixing my life with a magic wand. "But sadly, magic wands don't exist in the real world," I mumbled absentmindedly.

I sprang to my feet when the raven on the magnolia shrieked really loud in reply. I would have sworn it was trying to tell me that it didn't agree with my opinion.

Chapter 2

Alba

"So, Mrs. Andersson, tell me about your work experience."

The woman wore an expensive suit and was rattling nervously with her pencil, which had been engraved with the rubric *MSTDA Engineering*. I was probably the fifth candidate she was interviewing that day, and she was visibly fed up to the back teeth.

I swallowed, raking my mind for an elegant answer. I had an engineering degree, but my résumé was emptier than my spouse's heart. Back in the day when I still thought he cared for me, Mark had suggested I should find a more *ladylike* career—his words, not mine—away from slush-drenched boots, concrete and shadily shirtless construction workers. Maybe try to work from home, so I could take proper care of our family. Over the years, this had led me to many failed attempts to sell all sorts of useless things to my scarce and distant relatives, who had acquired some of that crap out of sheer pity. Now my parents were dead, and I still had a garage full of essential oils, sports apparel and allegedly natural cosmetics which had probably gone rancid in the meanwhile.

"I'm a civil engineer," I said in a quiet voice, my eyes fixed on the table. My pencil skirt, a remnant of long-gone office days, had become too tight around my waist after two kids, so I was trying to breathe as shallowly as possible, in case the zipper burst and poked the interviewer's eye out.

"Sorry for asking this question, but do you have any children?" she said, not looking sorry in the least.

"It's all right," I sighed. "I have two daughters. One is three, and the other is five years old."

She nodded, her lips pursing into a fine line as she wrote something into her file.

There we go again. Kids get sick all the time, and mothers miss work because of that. Particularly, soon-to-be-divorced mothers were a very much feared species among employers.

"I see," she continued, "Tell me, Mrs. Andersson, why do you want this position?"

A simple question I didn't feel like answering, frankly.

"Because my soon-to-be-ex-husband is an elite solicitor who has threatened to use all his knowledge and connections to rob me of everything I own and love."

The truth somehow didn't sound right, so I sugarcoated it a bit, "I have been idle for too long, and I miss feeling useful to society," I uttered proudly. "I used to work for Reismann and Reismann, and I enjoyed that job very much."

The woman raised an eyebrow.

"You mean the Reismann and Reismann that closed down five years ago?"

"That one, yes," I answered with a sigh.

"And after that?"

I remained silent. What was I supposed to say? *"I sold essential oils on a godforsaken website?" "I nagged all my neighbors to buy moisturizer from me?"*

"I was a stay at home mom," I said, shrugging, well-aware of the repelling effect this answer usually had on interviewers. This wasn't my first interview after

Mark's divorce notice, and not even the worst one.

I glanced around the sleek and sterile office, with large floor-to-ceiling windows which overlooked Emberbury's modestly sized business district. My stomach rumbled, reminding me that I hadn't eaten anything since dinner, apart from a few spoonfuls of mushy cornflakes the kids had left in their bowls after breakfast. I had given instructions to the nanny, spent one hour trying on corporate clothes that were too tight or out of fashion, or lacked buttons, then jumped into a taxi; all of that just to be left to wait for forty-five minutes in a waiting room and be asked how many children I had and why the company I used to work for had been closed for more than five years.

The interviewer's cell phone rang, and she excused herself. I stood up and admired the view of the city: we were on the eighteenth floor, and for someone like me, used to living in a suburban home, the feeling was akin to traveling by plane. Tall glass skyscrapers reflected the early morning sun, blinding me. Many feet down, people walked, all in a hurry and all minding their own business.

All except for two.

There were two men dressed in black right in front of the entrance to *MSTDA Engineering*, and they were both looking up in my direction. I recoiled as a strange energy buzzed over the back of my neck. I'd seen them somewhere before, but where? After a second, I shook my head. There was no way they could be watching me through the mirror glass, especially when I was so high above them. The situation with Mark was starting to get to me, and I had begun to see danger behind every corner.

When the interviewer came back, she went through a couple more customary questions, then checked her watch, widened her eyes with feigned surprise and opened the door for me.

"Time's up, but thank you for your time, Mrs. Andersson," she said, waving me towards the exit. "We will let you know about our decision very quickly."

Probably as quickly as one could write the word "rejected."

***

Walking in broad daylight, I strained to focus on my fellow pedestrians and traffic lights but couldn't help shambling like a drunk ostrich. The problem was that I could only focus on one thought: how was I going to keep my children if Mark was determined to use all his powers to take them away from me?

After finding out what had happened to his favorite shirt, Mark had been oddly calm. I had expected a storm, but he had embraced my audacity with a single evil smirk.

"I thought you'd like to know that I'm going to fight for custody of the girls," he had said, the smile never leaving his lips as he unbuttoned his double cuffs. "Those post-partum depression records… and all that yelling, you know… I think they'd be safer staying with me three weeks out of four… or just permanently, don't you think? That way, you'd have enough time to sort out your deeply messed up existence. *And hair.*"

Always a beautiful remark from him.

Mark had never expressed much interest in child rearing, so his suggestion could only have one explanation: he hated me so much that he had decided to sink me. But why? When I had met him, he had been all charm and attentions. But then, his charismatic façade had slowly collapsed. Behind closed doors, he had become nothing short of a monster.

I wondered how I would fight someone like him. And I didn't even have a job to cover the expenses.

A loud horn restored me to reality: I had just walked in front of a moving bus. The driver was yelling at me, his eyes almost bulging out of the sockets. I didn't blame him. I was so distracted that I hadn't even noticed stepping over the curb.

I had to pull myself together.

My first priority was finding a way to sustain myself until things became clearer; maybe an apartment in case he also took away the house as he had hinted. Even something temporary would do, just to start filling in that flagrantly blank résumé. I would get myself a good attorney—hopefully one who wasn't Mark's friend—and fight for custody of the kids.

He counted on me giving up, as always.

I was in the middle of my silent self-pep-talk when a big black bird crossed my path, blocking it.

That raven again. Those fiery, clever eyes were hard to miss. It had to be the same one that often loitered around our magnolia tree.

I tried to scare it off, but it just sat in the middle of the sidewalk. It didn't even bat an eyelid. Did ravens ever blink? And weren't they supposed to be afraid of scarecrows?

Seeing that the creature didn't intend to move, I decided to bypass it, shaking my head at its audacity.

I was about to keep walking towards the bus stop when I noticed that the bird was holding something shiny in its beak: it looked like a decently sized engagement ring.

My engagement ring!

"Wait!" I shouted, turning around towards the raven. But the bird took off and started to fly toward a nearby park.

"Hey, stop! Give that back!"

I ran after it, pushing away anyone who stood in my way and ignoring their surprised stares. The bird had stolen my engagement ring, which I had planned to pawn to get some backup money.

There was no way on earth I was allowing him to get away with that.

***

The raven flew across the street into a thicket of trees. I jumped over a tree stump just in time to avoid falling on my nose. The bird was faster than I, but just the thought of losing sight of that expensive ring was enough to make my legs gallop. I couldn't afford to lose such a valuable jewel just because of a stupid animal who had a fancy for sparkly things.

"Stop!" I yelled, not that I expected the bird to understand me. But oddly enough, the raven turned its head around and waited for me. "You thief! Give that back right now!"

I lifted my fist in anger. Oh, come on. This was unbelievable. I was not in a position to lose even one penny.

Then, my feet sunk into the ground. I stepped on what I thought was just a bunch of dry branches, but the ground gave way, and an invisible hole sucked me into the earth.

I fell.

I screamed until my lungs emptied of air.

Then my body smashed into the hard, cold ground. The darkness of the hole swallowed me, ushering me into unconsciousness.

**Continue reading *Stray Witch*
in eBook, paperback, or audiobook format.**

About the author

Eva Alton writes stories that blend humor, love, and (hopefully) unforgettable characters who linger in your heart long after you finish the book. With a style that combines the magical and the ordinary, her works offer readers moments of escapism, laughter, and reflection.

In her paranormal fiction, such as the popular series The Vampires of Emberbury and The Witches of Ibiza, Eva explores worlds where vampires, witches, and humans share their light and darkness, proving that monsters aren't always what we think. Her talent for crafting realistic characters and clever dialogue has made her a must-read author for fans of romantic urban fantasy.

In the romantic comedy genre, her Carpi Café series charms readers with hilarious and heartwarming stories about love, second chances, and the magic hidden in life's chaos. Between laughs, books, and cozy moments, these romcoms remind us that life's unexpected twists are often the best ones.

Eva also shares her expertise with aspiring writers through her Autorissimo project, offering resources and guides to help others bring their own stories to life.

P.S. If you've Eva's writing, you're welcome to explore her other books:

- The Vampires of Emberbury Series: You've just finished The Vampire's Assistant, a prequel to the series. Keep reading Stray Witch (book 1). (There's also a 4-book bundle, The Vampires of Emberbury.)
- Witches of Ibiza Series: Begins with Iris, The Witch's Bloodspell, and continues with Selena, Wolf Moon.
- Historical Fantasy: Hidden Notes, a novel weaving the Spanish Civil War with ghosts, European travel, and a lost treasure.
- Romantic Comedy: Check out my stories from the Carpi Café in Barcelona (Tales of Love and Lattes).

You're also welcome to Eva's weekly newsletter:

https://sendfox.com/evaalton

A small thank-you gift

Would you like to see a picture of Julia and Ludovic?

Scan the code and I'll send you a few illustrations to your email.

9 798201 957063